TESSILI
ACADEMY

BOOKS BY ROBIN STEPHEN

Chronicles of the Tessilari
Tessili Academy
Tessili Rogue
Tessili Revenge

Annals of the Brinlocks
Brinlin Isle
Brinlin Forest
Brinlin Cove

Tessili Academy

Chronicles of the Tessilari: Book I

A Story of Bydaira

Robin Stephen

This is a work of fiction. All characters, events, and organization portrayed in this novel are either product's of the author's imagination or are used fictitiously.

TESSILI ACADEMY

ISBN 978-0-9844912-5-4 (ebook)
ISBN 978-0-692-49838-5 (print)

Cover design by Robin Deutschendorf
Maps by Robin Deutschendorf

Brown Wing Press
Iowa City, IA
brownwingpress.com

First Brown Wing Press Edition

for my parents, for always
supporting my wildest dreams

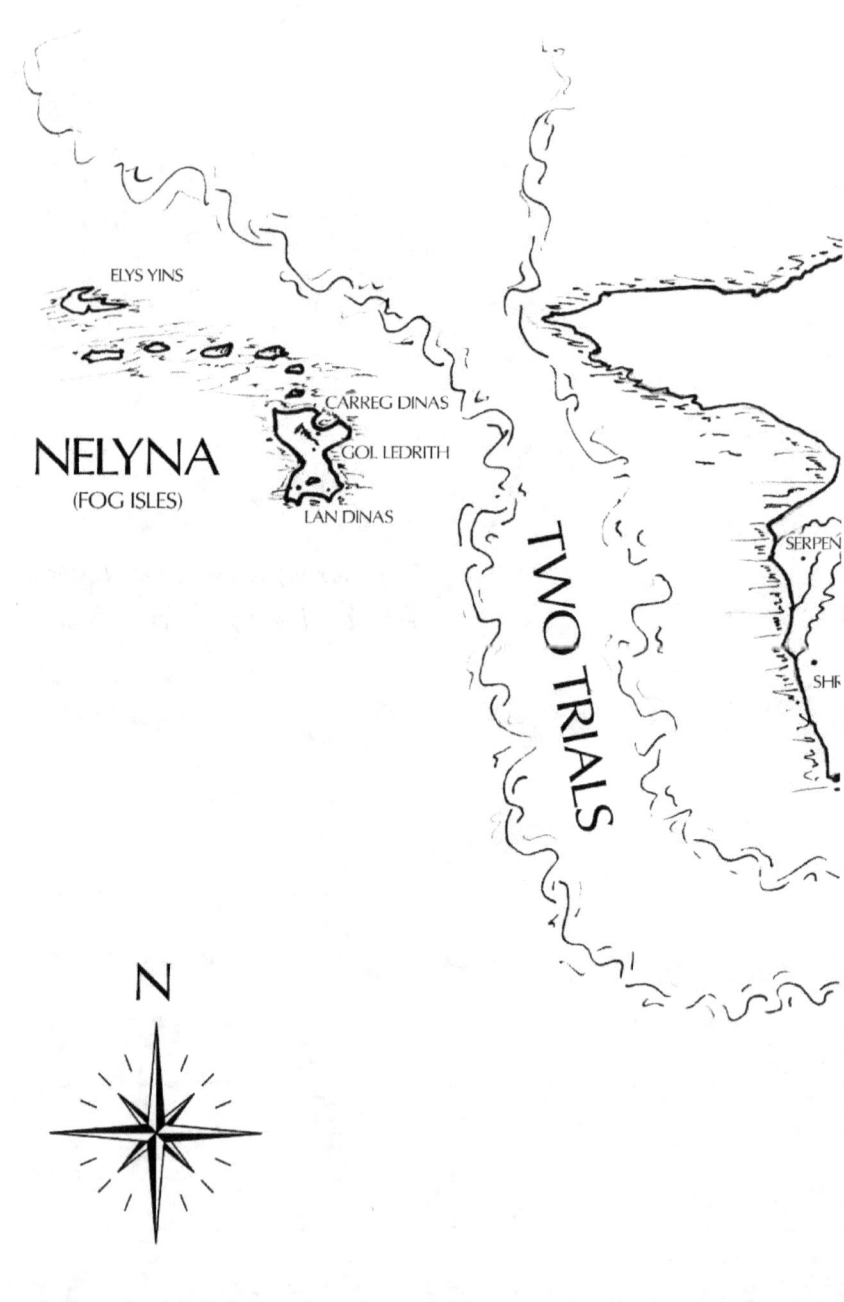

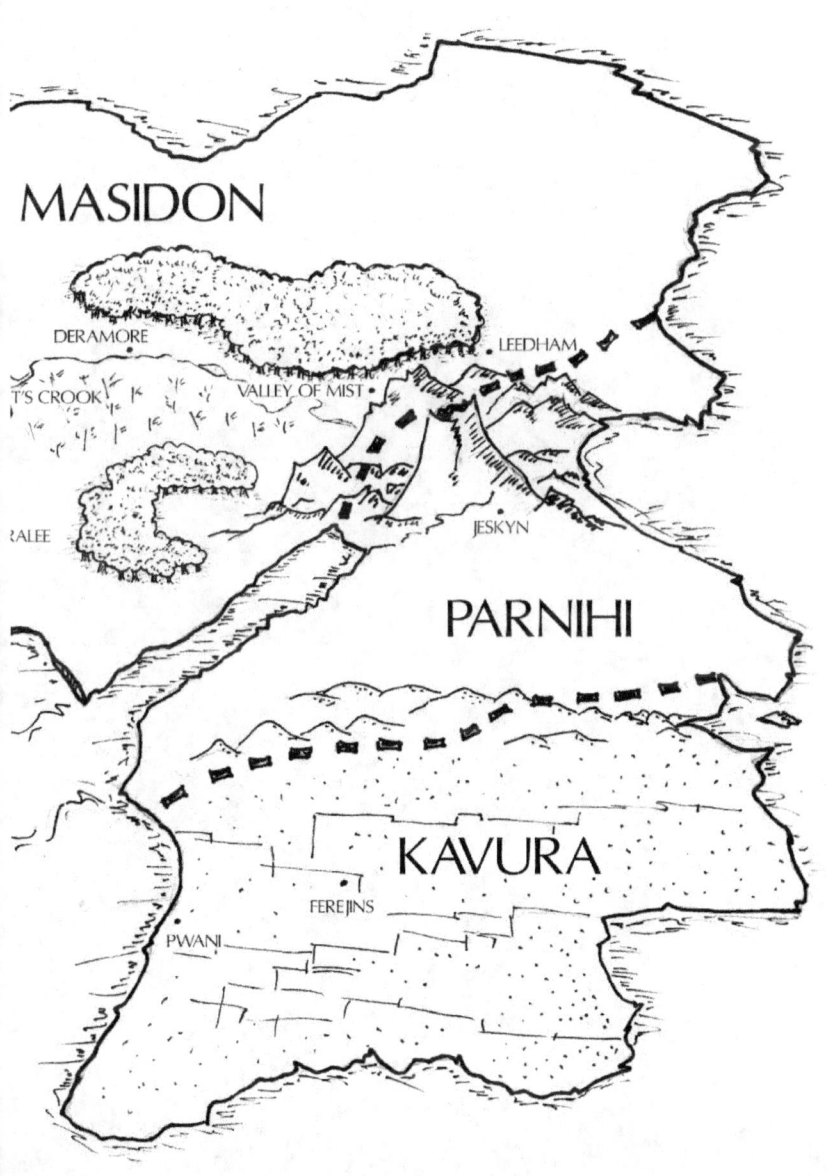

CHAPTER 1

Principal Frane and Dean Balist strode through the thriving quad. Sunlight fell on their faces, glinting off the silver threads spun into their robes. Around them, the academy was alive with life. Flowering brillbane grew along every walkway, attracting tessili to dart around the blooms like bright, delicate jewels.

Balist walked with his hands clasped behind his back, feeling pleased with his surroundings. Surely, the campus had not been so well-tended in centuries. Ever since he'd risen to his current station in Masidon and thus inherited the dean's position ten years before, he'd seen the gardens here attended to with particular devotion. And it showed.

The two men reached the murmuring central fountain. Balist paused for a moment to regard the shimmering shapes of the golden fish that shifted beneath the dancing surface of the water.

In the distance, three girls sat on one of the lawns. Their long skirts pooled around them like spilled milk.

As Frane and Balist stood looking on, one of the girls said something. The other two burst into bright laughter. Balist, too far away to have heard the joke, found himself smiling along with them anyway.

Frane, at Balist's elbow, spoke. "That's the one, sir. The one in the middle. I mentioned her in my report."

Balist felt the smile leave his face. The sun, warm and pleasant a moment before, suddenly seemed overly bright. He shielded his eyes with one narrow hand. "Frane," he said, "I spoke with Nylan. He disagrees with you. He told me she's our best. An early graduation for her would be a loss for the academy. Six more months won't make such a difference."

Frane was shorter than Balist. He had the reddish hair of the people of the Fog Isles, now shot with gray. He frowned as he listened to Balist's argument. Balist knew very little about the older man, other than he'd been the principal at the academy for longer than Balist had known of its existence. The man struck Balist as overly conservative. If it had been left up to Frane when graduation occurred, the academy would have hardly any students at all by now.

Frane made no reply. He squinted towards the girls. They were smiling, their tessili flying loops around their heads. They were such sweet things, Balist thought. They sat in the sun, their cheeks smooth, hair shining, the picture of health and ease. It was the one with the blonde hair and chocolate eyes that had Frane all worked up. Over nothing, Balist was certain.

Frane said, voice grim, "It's my job, sir, to watch out."

Balist set a hand on the older man's shoulder. Frane was thin, but the wiry sinews of his arm were taut beneath Balist's fingers. "And you do your job so well. Nylan said he'll submit a full assessment after her next opportunity. We'll see what the data say. Now, come on. I'm ready for lunch."

As they turned from the girls and continued across the courtyard, the flashnodes on the walls reached full brightness. It was hard to see their progress in the sun, but now they flared to brilliance, then went out. Balist glanced over his shoulder one last time, noting how all three girls had gone still as statues. It always fascinated him, the way that worked.

For a moment, the quad was silent. The colorful tessili continued to fly, but otherwise the scene was still. For several heartbeats, it remained so. Then, one of the girls spoke. Her voice was distant, tone vague.

Balist turned away. As he waited for Frane to work the complex lock that would let them off student grounds, he felt a momentary pang of sadness for what was to come – for what always came, at the end of each year. Then, Frane swung the door aside. Balist stepped into the domed exit hall, feeling a mild relief to be out of the sun.

◈

Jey ran her fingers through Elle's long, dark hair. On the other side of the room, Kae sat at her desk, doodling with a loose ink pen as her brilliant green tessila chased the nib and nudged it this way and that, adding hiccups to what would have been smooth, flowing lines.

Outside the tall windows, the sun was dropping. The light was growing warm and rich. Soon the academy walls would throw their long shadows over the dorms.

Jey's tessila, scarlet hide brilliant in the late light, clung to the swaying sleeve of her dress. He grasped the fabric with his tiny talons as it moved with the rhythmic motion of Jey's hands.

Elle leaned back against Jey's legs, eyes closed. She hummed a vague tune while her purple tessila lay stretched out full length on her thumb, wings drooping in contented relaxation.

Jey's fingers continued their dance. Elle hummed. Jey found herself humming as well. She seemed, somehow, to know the tune.

She reached the bottom of the braid and tied it off with a golden ribbon. "What are you humming?" The room was quiet, the cloister still around them. It seemed to Jey the academy had once been crowded. Now it was silent all the time. She remembered, when she'd been young, seeing classes of six or seven girls. Now, every class seemed smaller than the last. She, Elle, and Kae were the only seniors. Younger classes had two members mostly, or sometimes just one.

"My mother used to sing that song." Elle's voice was drowsy as she spoke, but Jey felt a strange little stab. *Mother.* The word gripped her heart like an invisible claw.

Out of reflex, Jey glanced at the flashnode tucked discreetly up near the ceiling. But the light was dim, the bulb not yet a quarter full. They had time.

At her desk, Kae had stopped doodling. She turned, setting down her pen, which her tessila nudged and sent rolling across the spattered paper. Kae stopped it with an idle hand and said, in a bemused, distant voice, "Mine too."

The three of them stared at each other. Jey felt something rise up in her, some strange feeling of knowing something she did not know. She looked down, frowning. She noted the ribbon at the end of the braid she'd made was crooked. She untied it to redo the bow. As her fingers brushed the delicate contours of Elle's neck, a thought surfaced in her mind. *One hand on the throat, the other on the base of the skull. Now push.* In her mind's eye, Jey seemed to see a flash of light. She felt the memory of an exhilarating rush inside her own head. *I could kill her, just like that.*

The thought shocked her into sitting back. The ribbon fell from her fingers. The braid began to uncoil, the ends unwinding in lazy loops. Jey shot out of her chair and hurried to the counter, where the spritzer sat. She gripped the hollow crystal base and inserted the golden nozzle into her nose. She squeezed the white balloon in one hand. A mist shot out of the nozzle. She sucked it in.

Immediately, the thoughts faded. Her mind turned soft and blank. She let out a deep sigh. *It's been happening more and more lately.* But the thought had no power. It faded like a dream.

"Anyone else?" Jey said, turning back to face the room, spritzer in one hand. Elle had sat up and was completing the work of unwinding her braid. Kae's eyes had the stunned look Jey recognized too well. "Both of you," she said, setting the spritzer in Kae's hand. "Come on. And Elle, stop humming, will you?"

As Kae accepted the spritzer, Jey lifted the dangling end of her long, white sleeve. She remembered how, long ago, she had looked at the seniors and envied them their pure white dresses. Now, her tessila was brilliant against the pale folds of fabric. She raised her sleeve so he was level with her eye. She held him there for a moment.

Diminutive as he was, he stared back at her with his dark, fierce eyes. Unafraid.

She heard Kae inhale, then pass the spritzer to Elle. *It takes more each week.* But again, the thought was nothing. It was as pale as a shadow in the moonlight, and meant even less.

◈

Jey hurried out of the rooms she shared with Elle and Kae, pulling the door closed until she heard the click of the latch. The dorm cloister was deserted, all the other students off at class already.

Jey was running late. She was running late because her tessila had hidden from her that morning. He'd been doing that with some frequency lately. When she'd found him at last, tucked underneath a quill, he'd hissed when she'd picked him up. Now he sat in the curl of her hand, inert, refusing to climb up her sleeve or stow himself anywhere more convenient.

The morning light was pale. The delicate columns threw shadows over the shrubbery and lawn that occupied the cloister's center. She hurried down the south walkway. It was cool in the shadows – too cool for the tessili to have come courting the flowers.

Jey had nearly reached the set of double doors that lead to the quad when a small shape darted through them and all but ran into her. Startled, Jey jumped back, clutching the hand that held her tessila protectively to her chest.

The girl, for it was a girl, wore the dark dress of a pre-initiate. She dodged to one side, ran past Jey, and hurried onto the lawn to dive under one of the brillbane bushes. Before Jey could decide what this might mean, ringing footsteps sounded around the corner. Professor Dail strode into view, his face rigid with frustrated impatience. He saw Jey standing in the cloister doorway. "Have you seen anyone? A girl? B412? She ran out of my classroom not a minute ago."

Jey didn't know why she did it. Lying was an affront to Priam, the god of honor. She'd been taught from her earliest days never to do it. Jey didn't know if she'd ever lied before. If she had, she couldn't remember. Now, the words slipped out of their own accord, "No, sir."

Her tessila chose that moment to emerge, poking his narrow head from the cave of her fingers. Professor Dail looked at her, eyes flicking from her face to her tessila, then back again. He seemed to weigh her with his hooded eyes. Then he turned away, heading up the walkway that led towards the center of the quad and the fountain.

Feeling a strange thrill, Jey made her way to the bush. Mindful of her white skirts, she crouched and peered underneath the waxy branches. The girl was not very well hidden. The bush was too dense to let her in much. Her small feet weren't even in shadow. Jey could hear her quick, ragged breath and smell the sweet musk of the brillbane blooms.

Jey didn't know what to say, so she said nothing. She reached under the bush and gave the girl's bare ankle a quick, gentle squeeze. Then she stood and walked a few paces away to settle herself on one of the stone benches that stood on the grass, soaking in the weak morning sun.

It took only a moment for the girl to emerge. She was a thin child, no older than five, with huge bright eyes and hair that needed to be rebraided. She scrambled out from under the bush and flung herself at Jey. Her dress was askew. She'd lost a slipper. Startled, Jey caught her, her tessila leaping from her hand to fly in an agitated loop around her head. The child, warm and heavy, collapsed against her legs. Jey held her, feeling the deep, silent sobs that racked the small body.

Jey let her cry. She seemed to recall crying like this herself from time to time, though she couldn't think why she might have done such a thing. She stroked the disarrayed hair and waited.

After a time, the girl's sobbing quieted. She sniffled. Jey was aware she was quite late by now, and perhaps her dress was mussed as well. She said, "Your name is Bea?"

The girl was kneeling on the ground, leaning against Jey's legs. Now she separated herself and glared up with red-rimmed eyes. "My name is Frani." Her tone was fierce. "I want my mother."

Something stirred deep inside Jey's mind. She seemed to hear an echo, seemed to recall her own childish voice saying those exact words. *I want my ....* *My name is ....*

Her tessila landed on her shoulder and made his slinking way down her sleeve, pausing to regard the girl with his brilliant eye. The child went very still at the sight of him. "Do you have your tessila yet?" Jey knew she did not, of course, but it seemed an easy way to change the subject.

The girl shook her head. "I want one, though."

Jey found herself reciting part of the sermon Peia Garot had delivered on Apex. "Delari, the goddess of bounty, brings us what we are prepared to receive."

The girl's small brows lowered, but she said nothing. Then the sound of footsteps rang through the quiet cloister. The girl flinched, half turning as three orderlies strode in from the quad. Professor Dail had called for reinforcements.

"Ah, you found her," one of the young men said. The three stepped onto the lawn.

For a moment, Jey feared the girl would run again. But she only sat, hollow eyed, as the men drew near. Two of them stopped a few paces away while the third continued forward. He crouched down in the grass, fumbling in the pouch at his waist. He brought out the small, glass tube of a single dose spritzer. He held it to the girl's nose. Suddenly docile, the child didn't resist. He squeezed the plunger, she inhaled the mist. He patted the girl's hand. "There now, Bea. Let's get you cleaned up."

The orderly stood, straightening his tan robes. He glanced at Jey, but said nothing. Jey remembered, with a strange, surprised rush, her own orderly. Like this man, he'd been young, with light hair and a shy smile. She felt a strange tug in her chest. She couldn't remember the last time she'd seen him, or what his name had been.

Bea wiped her eyes and rose to her feet. The sun was growing warmer now. Jey was aware she should get to class. She watched the girl walk across the grass, one foot bare, the other slipper stained with damp dirt. As two of the orderlies split off and headed back to the quad, Bea and the third man disappeared through the heavy doors that led into the initiate's hall.

Jey stood, smoothing her dress. As she turned to go, she spotted the missing slipper at the base of a column. She walked to it and picked it up. It was soft and light in her hand.

She was about to follow the girl and her orderly, to return the slipper, when the flashnode at the top of the column went off. Its brilliant light flared in Jey's eyes.

Her thoughts dissolved into white snow.

•••

Jey stood in the dorm cloister, holding a child's slipper in her hand. She stared at the object in mild wonder. She blinked, unable to imagine why she would have such a thing. She stood for a time, turning it over in her hands. It was so small. Her tessila crept down her arm, flicking his quick tongue at the embroidered side.

She was still standing like this when Professor Liam strode into the cloister. He walked through the propped open doors from the quad, glancing up and down the long space until he saw her. Then he took a few quick strides in her direction. "Jey." His tone was impatient. "What are you…" He broke off, taking in the dull flashnode above her head and the small slipper in her hand.

Professor Liam closed his eyes for one long heartbeat. "Delari, grant me patience." He muttered the words under his breath. Then he approached. Gently, he took the slipper and set it on a nearby bench. He wrapped his warm, firm fingers around her wrist. He gave her a small tug. "It's time for class now, Jey."

When she didn't move, he fell back beside her. He set a hand on the small of her back. He guided her forward, though she resisted at first. It seemed to Jey there was something she should remember.

All around her, the cloister was quiet. The columns threw their long shadows. One or two early tessili stirred in the bushes. *I want my …. My name is ….*

But the thoughts faded. By the time they reached the doors to the quad, Jey was moving on her own energy. A few steps later, Professor Liam let his hand fall away. They walked together, not speaking, towards his classroom.

◈

Jey woke to a hand on her shaking her shoulder. She opened her eyes and knew she was not in her own room.

"Get up now, girl. It's time for your opportunity." The voice that spoke was a smooth, neutral tenor. Jey recognized it as belonging to Chim, one of the orderlies who attended Handler Nylan. Chim carried a candle. Its small flame danced and bobbed on its wick. Light pooled around the man's chest. The only other illumination in the room was the dull glow emitted by the flashnode in the corner. It was full, but did not flash. Which meant it must be disabled for the moment.

Jey sat up, recognizing the room now, too. It was in the small complex attached to the deployment blocks. She must have been instructed to sleep here instead of going to her dorm room.

She didn't remember this happening. But she was used to that.

Yawning in the dark room, Jey put on the clothing Chim handed her. A pair of dark leather leggings were tight to get on but conformed to her shape once she had them laced into place. A soft, clinging dark shirt and a dark leather vest went on top. As she pulled on her dark gloves, Chim hung a long dark cloak around her shoulders.

Chim took a moment to look her over, then picked up his candle and turned to open the door. Jey glanced around the room with a vain hope, but her tessila did not sneak out of some hiding place to follow her. He'd have been kept back in the academy. He always was when she had opportunities. She knew that. She could feel the dull ache in her chest that meant he was not near. She left the room slowly, heart heavy with dread.

Outside the room, a dim corridor stretched into the night. Chim moved quickly; Jey had to hurry to keep up. They walked past the closed doors of more sleeping chambers, then turned left.

Chim opened a door and held it for her. He waited, indicating she should go ahead.

Jey stopped walking. Something shifted in her chest. A thought rose, unbidden. *Don't go. Don't go in.*

"J114, get in here. And Chim, close that door." The words sounded in the room beyond the door in a tone Jey knew well.

Jey didn't move. Her heart was suddenly pounding. Her mouth had gone dry. *Run.* The thought quivered in her mind like a broken promise.

"Handler Nylan, you may need to help me here." Chim spoke in a careful, liquid tone. He removed a long, slim wand from within his robes and held it in his hand. It looked innocuous, but Jey knew it was not. "I don't think you want me to zap her right now."

Handler Nylan appeared in the doorway, his jaw set with irritation. His dark eyes raked over Jey in fierce displeasure.

Run. The thought came again. Jey quivered, but she couldn't move.

"Oh for the love of Priam." The Handler strode forward, grabbed Jey's arm, shoved her sleeve up beyond her elbow, and stabbed a needle into her flesh. He was so quick, so rough, Jey did not have time to react. As Nylan dipped the plunger, administering the injection, she saw the grid of silver scars on the soft skin of her inner elbow, arrayed like a small galaxy around the place where the needle pierced her skin. *From all the shots.*

Handler Nylan withdrew the needle and turned to Chim. "I can take it from here." The orderly tucked his stunrod back into his robes, and withdrew.

Jey stood, rooted to her spot. Something was happening. Her mind was clearing. Bit by bit, thoughts rose, surfacing one after another, like popping bubbles. She blinked, trying to contain it all as the old, fierce, familiar anger bloomed through her.

Handler Nylan was watching her. There was a lamp on the wall. His heartless eyes looked out at her from dark sockets. "Now, J114, would you like to hear about your opportunity, or will it be tonight that we kill your little beast?"

Jey closed her eyes in a rush of horrible understanding. She remembered now. She remembered everything. This was why they didn't let her bring her tessila with her. Tonight, he was a hostage, just as he had been so many times before. *Not my tessila,* she thought, *Phril. His name is Phril. This time, I* will *remember. I will remember at least that.*

CHAPTER 2

The opportunity was simple. Go to the house of a nobleman, break into his room, and change his mind on the subject of an upcoming vote that would be taken in the House of Laws. Then, on the way home, stop at a farm and make a young man fall out of love with a young woman. Jey received her assignments with the accompanying sense of relief that came whenever she realized she should be able to make it through her night's work without killing anyone.

She received her instructions in grim silence. She had followed Nylan through the door Chim had opened. On the other side was a deployment block. One wall of the large room was covered in an elaborate weapon's rack. A tall black horse with no white markings stood in front of a large double door, saddled and tied, straining a little on its rope to try to look back at them. The room was outfitted with all kinds of supplies, with everything from stout ropes and grappling hooks to elaborate metal and glass spectacles that would allow a person to see far into the distance. Jey could select anything she thought she might need and take it with her.

Now, Nylan turned to take a ring down from the wall. It seemed an innocuous thing, a slim band of pale silver. As she watched, Nylan gripped the ring in both hands and pulled, so the two halves separated. They came apart, but a line of blue energy continued to snake between the separated ends, dancing and writhing on the air. "The oath." He held the separated bracelet towards her.

Furious with herself for never being able to find a way out of this, Jey stuck her hand between the two halves. The blue light danced on the dark fabric of her shirt. She spoke the words she so hated.

> *I will fulfill my given task. I will not deviate from my path. I will seek to avoid all people. If I am spoken to, I will not respond. I will make no attempt to communicate with others using any method, or share with any living creature anything I may know. Once I have left this place, I will not pursue any other task, desire, or goal other than that which I have been given until I have returned.*

As Jey finished speaking, Nylan let his hands open. The two halves of the bracelet snapped back together, going solid around her wrist. Jey felt the shock as the spell took hold.

She glared at Nylan, making no attempt to hide the murder in her eyes. The irony of it was, it would be such a simple thing for her to kill him. It would take only a moment. They'd taught her the first half dozen ways to do it when she'd been ten years old.

Nylan seemed to sense what she was thinking. His grim face twitched into a dry smile. "You should thank me, J114. Tomorrow I intend to finish persuading Dean Balist not to move your graduation forward. That's six whole months of life you have me to thank for. You might consider showing a little gratitude, for once."

With a final, unpleasant twitch of his mouth, Nylan strode from the room, saying over his shoulder, "You have five hours."

◈

Whenever there was a light visible out in the deployment block complex, Professor Liam found it difficult to sleep. Tonight was no exception. It was a warm night, and breezy. They were at the apex of the year. He had the windows open, his chamber was stuffy with the heat.

Although Liam had tried several times to get into bed, he was up now, pacing around his chamber. Outside, the moon was a high, bright, and sliver. The grounds of the faculty complex were full of swaying shadows. Of course, no matter how hard he stared at the cobbled lane that ran away from the academy to the gate that opened to the bridge that crossed the river—the only way off the island—he never saw anyone coming or going on these nights. They were too good for that, these girls. A fact he was partly to thank for.

He thought of the girl, Jey, whom he'd found holding a child's slipper in the dorm cloister, standing there staring at it when she should have been in his classroom. Unlike many of the other professors, Liam called the girls by their letter, as their orderlies called them and they called themselves. Back when the academy had been full, there had been a fair bit of overlap. Now, it wasn't much of a problem.

He was worried about Jey. She was showing symptoms, little stirrings, signs she was learning to fight the drugs, the flashnodes, the elaborate lie that was the academy's daytime life. He knew the warnings, like everyone else who lived beside these girls, day to day. The cardinal gauge was simple: "The more the flashnodes affect them, the more dangerous they are."

He'd seen Jey today – still as stone, bemused, staring at that slipper as if she'd never seen one before. What had happened before he'd arrived? He didn't know – couldn't ask her.

Every year, he saw it with the seniors. The year they were to turn 18, the flashnodes tripped them up more and more, making them pause, disorienting them, disrupting them, turning them into slim, delicate statues with blank faces.

And then, every fall, there was a ceremony. The dean spoke. The younger girls attended. Diplomas were presented. Those girls, the dangerous ones, graduated.

But there were never any parents in attendance. And afterwards, if the girls left, they did so by some means Liam had never been able to discover.

Liam didn't know, precisely, what happened to them. But he had his suspicions. Because out beyond the bridge and the gates, off the island where the school stood in its isolated splendor, no graduate of Tessili Academy existed. As far as the world was concerned, this place didn't exist at all.

And Liam wasn't the only one who'd noticed the warning signs in Jey. A few days before, the Dean and Principle had come to his classroom asking if he thought Jey's timeline should be "accelerated." The question had made Liam sick. The words these men used. The blandness of the Dean's tone when he'd said, "We believe she might be a candidate for early graduation."

He'd answered their questions, not expressing an opinion one way or another. After all, he wasn't in a position to defend anyone.

Still, it weighed on him. It was June. Even if they didn't accelerate her, Jey had six months.

Liam leaned on the windowsill, staring out in the windblown darkness. In the distance, one of the hounds let out its high, lonely bay. He was not an old man. Not yet. But nights like this, he felt he carried the years of seven grandfathers.

◈

The sound of rattling cutlery startled Jey from a deep sleep. She rolled over, disoriented, strangely convinced she was somewhere other than her own room.

But then she saw Elle looking down at her, dark braid hanging over her shoulder. A tray sat on the bedside table, bearing a breakfast so fresh it was still steaming. Elle was smiling. "Lucky you. They gave you a free day." She tapped the silver medallion that hung in the place Jey's daily schedule would normally reside on a board above her desk. "High Orderly Fras sent this tray. He says you're to eat now, even if you go back to sleep after."

Jey smiled up at her friend, mumbling her thanks. By Delari, she was tired. She had to struggle to sit up, to select a warm roll and crack it open. As the sweet smell of fresh bread wafted up into her nostrils she felt her stomach growl, clawing inside her like a caged tessila.

The thought made her look around the room in sudden, vague worry. She caught a glimmer of red out of the corner of her eye. The tip of a red tail dangled from a notch in her headboard. It was one of her tessila's favorite places to hide when he was feeling sulky. *He's been sulky a lot lately.* The thought formed, and made her go still. There was something about him, her tessila, that she should remember. *He's been …. He is ….*

On the other side of the room, Kae was stepping into her slippers. "I think if one of us gets a free day, we should all get one." Kae was a heavy sleeper and would miss breakfast daily if her roommates didn't force her out of bed.

Jey picked up the small, rounded knife that lay on the tray and dipped it into a dish of spun butter. The butter melted as she spread it onto the warm bread.

Elle had been about to return to her own preparations, but she frowned, turning back to Jey. With one of her slim fingers, she pushed the sleeve of Jey's night dress a little further up her arm, revealing a long, shallow gash. "Oh Jey," the other girl said. "What happened?"

Jey went still again at the sight of her arm. A thought struggled to surface. *He was waiting in the lord's bedchamber. He knew I would be coming. He ….*

The thought broke off, but Jey's heart was hammering. Elle and Kae were both staring at her with evident concern. Jey seemed to hear hoofbeats, feel the rise and fall of a horse moving under her. But that was silly. She hadn't ridden a horse since … since ….

The flashnode in the corner of the room went off.

•••

Jey blinked and set the butter knife on the plate. As she moved, the sleeve of her night dress fell into place. It had been pushed up her arm for some reason. She put the warm bread into her mouth, sighing as the curling hunger in her stomach began to calm.

Elle turned away and walked to the mirror above the washbasin where she straightened her hair. Kae looked up from donning her slippers, a frown creasing her high forehead when she noticed the silver medallion on Jey's schedule board. "No fair," she said. "Why do you get a free day?"

◈

Professor Liam's classroom was one of Jey's favorite places. It was a large room with elaborate windows, the ceiling vaulted stone. It seemed to her she had once attended Liam's classes with other students, but today she was here alone.

Her tessila was in good spirits this morning. He darted around the room in lazy loops, sometimes stopping to hover above the bobbing flowers of the potted brillbane that stood before the windows. Two orderlies sat in a corner, notebooks open in front of them as they observed.

Professor Liam, who'd been sorting papers on his desk, now looked up at her. Liam was a tall man, with square shoulders and eyes that always struck Jey as both sad and kind. His hair was gray at the temples and sideburns. He looked at Jey now, keeping his eyes on her for a long time. Jey looked down at her notebook, embarrassed for some reason she couldn't define. Professor Liam released a short sigh. He strode forward. "Please place your tessila on the holdstone."

Jey looked for her tessila. Sensing her desire, he came darting through the air, red hide bright in contrast to the gray stone. He alighted on her hand. As she felt the gentle grip of his tiny talons, Jey was suffused with a sense of love so great it took her breath away. She stared at the small creature for a moment. His small body was warm. Though he was no longer than her thumb, he had a presence that somehow filled her mind.

Gently, she moved her hand towards the small, gray stone that sat at the edge of her desk. It was an unremarkable piece of rock, worn smooth and round. For a moment she thought she could remember sitting with similar stones, seeking out inconsistencies, rubbing them down with grit paper.

The thought faded. Her tessila stepped off her finger and settled onto the stone. His sinuous tail wrapped around its base. He set his sharp chinned face on the lip. His tongue flicked out once, twice. He folded his wings, content.

Jey looked up as Professor Liam approached her desk. He stopped quite close, closer than usual. He reached out to take the hand she'd used to place her tessila on the holdstone. She felt a little shock at his touch. She remembered something else. Something to do with a slipper, his hand on the small of her back.

She frowned. It made no sense. And she was distracted by what Professor Liam did next. With his other hand he pushed the white sleeve of her dress up a little, to reveal her forearm.

There was a gash there, shallow and broad. It was long, nearly reaching from the crook of her elbow to her wrist. Professor Liam stared down at it, frowning. "This was not made by a weapon."

Jey frowned too, staring at her marred skin. The edges of the wound gleamed, giving off a pale blue sheen. Professor Liam saw this, too. He tipped his hand this way and that, causing her arm to shift in the light from the tall windows.

Professor Liam pulled her sleeve back up into position. He set her hand on the table. He turned away, walking towards his own desk. "Do you not remember the passive shield spell I taught you? Were you not wearing one?"

Jey let her eyes drift half closed. It was always so hard, so strange, when her tessila was on the holdstone. It was as if her mind grew very slow, and very deep.

Professor Liam waited with the air of someone not expecting a quick answer. At last, she said, "It's tiring. Besides, no one ever attacks with magic."

Professor Liam turned to look at her again. His deep eyes were troubled. "But someone did." He said this in a tone that suggested he was speaking to himself rather than her. Finally, with a sigh, he said, "We will practice. We'll practice holding a passive shield in place for a length of time."

Jey couldn't stifle a dispirited moan. Nevertheless, she began to weave the spell, imagining the fabric of it in her mind. "But," Professor Liam continued before she was done, "to make it a little easier, cast it on your tessila. Not yourself. And hold it until our next session." He paused, looking at her. He added in a low mumble, "If you can, anyway."

Jey adjusted her spell based on his instructions. She'd practiced casting spells on her tessila before, of course. He never seemed to mind. It would make holding it a good deal easier. He was, after all, quite small.

In the corner, one of the orderlies yawned. Jey closed her eyes, put the final touches on her spell, and looped its weave over her tessila. He didn't fight it. She snugged it close around him and opened her eyes to see Professor Liam staring at her with a look so intense it made her jump a little.

"Tomorrow," he said, "we'll see how you've done."

With that, Professor Liam strode from the classroom, withdrawing into the small attached office. The two orderlies stood as well, collecting their notes and stretching as if they had sat through a long and boring class instead of a very brief one. Jey consulted her timepiece and her schedule. She saw with surprise she had quite a long time before her next class, which was with Professor Straph. She felt a strange reluctance to move. *No flashnodes in classrooms.*

She looked down at the red curl of her tessila's body. She felt that stirring in her heart again, something sweet and deep.

The orderlies were making their way across the room. "Come on, now, Jey," one of them said in his smooth, soft voice. "Class is dismissed."

Jey rose with reluctance, holding out her hand for her tessila to come onto. He'd had his eyes closed. Now he opened one, cocked his head, and released a brief, soft hiss. Startled, she glared down at him. "Come on, Phril," she whispered. "We have to go."

A moment passed before Jey registered what she'd said. *His name is …. This time, I will remember at least that.*

Jey's heart began to beat faster. The orderlies were closer now. Somehow Jey knew it was very, very important they not see her tessila showing signs of rebellious behavior. Once or twice, there had been little girls – girls whose tessili had not done as they were told.

Those girls were gone.

Jey's tessila stepped off the holdstone and onto her hand. Her chain of thought snapped. She turned and took a few quick steps to stay ahead of the orderlies as they moved towards the door.

◈

Professor Straph lunged at Jey, whirling his staff towards her head in a long, smooth arc. Jey rolled to the side, executed a graceful tumble, and popped up again beside him. But Professor Straph had anticipated her. He reversed the direction of his swing. The edge of his staff caught her in the shoulder. He pulled the blow and her shirt was padded, but the impact threw her off balance. She stumbled, losing the fluidity of her movement. On the holdstone at the edge of the sparring area, Phril hissed.

Jey scrambled to reset herself. She took a few steps backwards and settled into a ready stance, her weight balanced evenly between her two feet, her muscles relaxed but ready. She drew in a long, slow breath and waited for Professor Straph to come at her again.

Except, he didn't. While she had moved away, the lean man had set the end of his staff on the ground. Now he stood looking at her with his dark eyes. "You're distracted, J114." His voice was low and smooth, difficult to hear if you weren't paying enough attention. "And your tessila is restless."

Phril, Jey thought. *His name is Phril.*

It had been an hour since she'd left Professor Liam's classroom. She'd taken a walk around the quad, hoping to settle herself and her tessila both. She'd stood beneath a flashnode and waited for it to fill and go off. It hadn't helped. *I can remember.* The time between her lesson with Professor Liam and this moment was whole – a complete, unbroken block of memory.

Jey felt as if she'd found herself on a road. Although her shoes were worn with walking, though she carried a pack and clothing, when she looked back there was only a sheer cliff face with a thousand foot drop into empty, fog filled sky. The road continued ahead of her, but it did not go back.

She bowed her head. "My apologies, master. Professor Liam has asked me to see how long I could hold a spell. It's distracting for me, and uncomfortable for Ph … for my tessila." She tried to take deep breaths, to keep her eyes soft. She knew things, things Straph himself had taught her, about how to make her body suggest to others it was harmless. That she was harmless. She called upon that knowledge now.

Professor Straph's eyes sharpened. He took a step towards her and looked into her face. Although her mind was racing, Jey forced her gaze to relax. He was near enough she could smell the sandalwood scent of his soap. "When was your class with Liam?"

She pretended it took her some time to find the answer. She let her eyes slide partway shut. "Just before yours." This had the benefit of being true, even if it was misleading. Liam had used only a few minutes of their lecture hour, but if Straph checked her schedule, he would see her period with Liam had ended five minutes before she'd arrived here.

Straph spent another moment looking at her through his narrowed eyes. Then he turned and moved away, walking like a cat on his quick feet.

Cat. The word had appeared in her mind, unbidden. And now, like the path, she couldn't seem to attach it to anything. *What is a cat?*

She had only a moment to wonder. Straph reset his grip on the staff and whirled it towards her head.

CHAPTER 3

Jey left the washroom and joined the ranks of girls drifting towards the dining hall. She watched the other students. They all seemed to wander rather than walk, moving with a strange, dreamy lack of purpose Jey tried to emulate.

Phril rode on the ledge of her collarbone, looking around with his bright, dewdrop eyes. She could feel he was excited. She could also feel the weaving of her spell on him. It was still in place. Over the course of the day, it had grown easier to leave it there, easier not to think about it. It occupied a corner of her mind, but it grew more comfortable as the time passed.

And time did pass. Time passed, and Jey could remember. Classes had been dismissed for the day. All the girls were being shepherded towards the dining hall. Orderlies moved among them in tan robes, encouraging the flow with soft words or light touches on shoulders or backs.

For the girls did not move with any sort of purpose. Every now and then one of them stopped, going still to look vaguely out over the green expanse of the quad. The younger girls, in their blue gowns, did this the most often. The older girls, in silver, moved with more confidence.

Up ahead, Jey could make out two white gowns, bright against the tones of blue and silver around them. Elle and Kae moved like the others, drifting along with the general flow.

Ahead of them, girls filed through the doors to the dining hall. Jey was near the end of the group. She and a few other girls, one blue, two silver, were passing below a column when the flashnode at its top went off.

Jey froze, but she did so out of reflex. Around her, the other girls reacted as well. The one in blue faltered, her steps lagging. The orderly at their elbow guided her forward and through the doors.

The two in silver stopped walking entirely. There were only two orderlies outside now. They stood next to the doors, waiting to close them. Jey glanced at the blank, vacant looks on the other girls' faces and tried to imitate it. She stood in place like they did, eyes wide and glassy.

One of the two orderlies released an annoyed sigh. "For the love of Priam." The orderly's tone was low and quick with frustration. "This is a ridiculous place for one of those rotting things. And today with a senior right next to it."

The other orderly didn't reply, only gave a small, nonchalant shrug. He moved forward to one of the silver girls, speaking to her in a low tone, nudging her shoulder to encourage her forward. She seemed stuck for a moment. At last, she moved. The other girl in silver went with her.

Jey hesitated, uncertain how quickly she should pretend to recover. *They do something.* The thought raced through her head in a frantic effort to understand. *The flashnodes do something to our minds.*

The other orderly approached Jey, gripping her wrist to try to pull her forward. She resisted more out of reflex than a decisive desire not to move.

"Too much force." These words were spoken by the orderly who'd shrugged. He was a smooth faced man, with thin limbs and the hint of belly beneath his robes. He turned from shepherding the two silver girls into the dining hall. With surprising dexterity, he took a few quick steps forward and rapped the other orderly on the wrist. The first orderly gave a sharp grunt and released his grip.

Jey let her head list to one side to get a better look at him. Where the other orderly had a soft look to him, this one was different. He had a rugged look to his face. His palm had been rough against her wrist. He was young, his shoulders square with muscle.

The older orderly spoke. "You must be soft, smooth, gentle at all times, most especially if you touch one and her tessila is on her person"

Phril had indeed bridled at the orderly's behavior. Jey could see the red smudge of his form out of the corner of her eye. He'd raised his head and had his small, beaked mouth open, his wings flared, as if he could somehow drive the orderly away.

The younger orderly looked at Phril with a look of distaste. In fact, he looked angry. Some fierce spark burned deep within his eyes.

The older orderly saw this too. He took a step closer to the young man, so close their shoulders almost touched. He spoke in a low whisper, but his tone was firm and menacing. "Listen to me, man. One of these girls is a thousand times more valuable than you. Get one of them rattled and I promise you they'll have removed you by morning. I don't know how you arrived here, but I assure you we all followed the same path. Some of us live with what happened. Some get angry. If you choose anger, you choose your own end."

With these words, the older orderly turned back to Jey. For a moment, she felt a vague bloom of recognition. She seemed to recall his face, a younger version, smiling at her.

"Come now, Jey," he said. She took a tottering, uncertain step towards him. He set a gentle hand on her shoulder. "That's right. It's dinner time." His voice was smooth and soothing. She understood she knew this man – had known him for a long time. But she didn't know his name.

Jey let herself be guided into the dining hall as the younger man, seething with quiet anger, closed the large doors.

◈

It was dark and quiet in the senior's dorm. The windows were open. A night breeze sighed through the large space. Jey lay in her bed, listening to the cadence of Elle and Kae breathing as they slept.

Phril was on one of the brillbane bushes that grew in large, earthenware pots set about the room. He'd burrowed his way into a husk and was gnawing his way through the sweet rind on a seed sack. Jey could feel his simple pleasure with the undertaking.

Jey was not as relaxed as her tessila. She had emulated Elle and Kae as they'd brushed out their hair, donned their night dresses, and climbed into their plush beds. But Jey had not been able to get to sleep. She'd been lying awake for hours now.

The only light in the room came from the flashnode set into the domed ceiling. As she lay in tense wakefulness, she watched it fill slowly with light, then flare in a sudden, silent detonation. It did this, on average, twice an hour – though sometimes it seemed to fill a little slower or more quickly than usual.

Jey had followed Professor Liam's instructions. The spell she'd cast on Phril still clung to him, an invisible weave of protective magic. The strange thing was Jey now couldn't understand *how* she'd done it. She could remember Professor Liam telling her to cast the spell – could remember doing so without any particular confusion or difficulty. But now, if she tried to cast the same spell on anything else it was impossible. It was like trying to remember how to fly.

Somewhere out in the night, an owl hooted. *Owl.* The word popped into her head like "cat" had earlier in the day, but both words were the same, devoid of attachment to any meaning.

There was a soft click. The door to their room opened on silent hinges. Jey felt her heart begin to race. She forced her eyes closed, forced her face into a smooth mask, forced her body to go slack and still.

An orderly padded into the room. He moved on soft feet. First, he stepped into the alcove where Elle's bed was tucked against the wall. A moment later, he emerged and went into Kae's. At last, his soft feet approached Jey's bed.

It was so difficult not to move – yet somehow Jey knew betraying the fact she was awake could be disastrous.

She heard the rustle of robes as the orderly approached her bedside. A moment later, a smooth, cool palm rested briefly against her forehead. It sat there for a moment, gentle on her skin.

Jey focused on the muscles in her face, on keeping them relaxed, preventing her eyelashes from fluttering. The hand was removed from her forehead. There was a clink and a puff of air. A fine mist drifted down over Jey's face. She breathed in the familiar mist produced by a spritzer.

The orderly lingered a moment longer, then he moved on. She heard him set the spritzer bottle down, heard him pin their schedules to the boards above their desks. A moment later, the soft click of the closing door suggested he was gone.

It was the third time an orderly had checked on them in the night. Jey hadn't known anyone came into their room when they slept. But then, up until yesterday she hadn't known anything.

◈

"Back straighter, V567. E236, to flow through the turn you need more energy in that preparatory step. Orderly Cam, relax your arm. She's a girl, not a tiger."

Professor Tucram provided these instructions in an endless litany, directing them at various couples as he moved among them in the dance hall. A narrow, spindly man, he walked on light, delicate feet. He carried a short cane with him as he wove through the dancers, executing his own elaborate series of steps to stay out of everyone's way.

He used the cane at intervals to touch a shoulder, lift a hand on a back, or otherwise correct something about the posture or movement of his students.

A light sheen of sweat had broken out on Jey's forehead. It was a warm, bright morning, and her head was fuzzy from her sleepless night. It was extra hard, she was finding, to emulate the blank, passive behavior of her classmates when her mind felt dull with fatigue.

The dance they were practicing was an intricate variation of one that had been popular last season. Jey had stumbled several times as her orderly dance partner led her through the steps. She felt clumsy and thick-headed. Every time she deviated from the pattern, she felt conspicuous.

Phril was dozing. He sat with the other tessili. They occupied the holdstones that sat in a line on a slim table at the top of the hall. Phril didn't care much for the dance classes. He disliked the orderly touching Jey for so long and resented that sometimes she got quite far away from him, as the hall was long. He was not allowed to follow because he needed to remain on the holdstone.

The dance class was nearly over. Jey felt as exhausted as if she'd spent the entire hour executing sprints. She knew the dance, somehow. Judging from what Professor Tucram said, she'd learned it last year, as had all the other girls. She moved through the steps easily enough, but she could not remember learning it, couldn't say how she knew to move her feet or lean her body this way or that, responding to the light pressure of the orderly's hand on her palm or waist.

Jey had spent much of the night trying to fit the pieces together, trying to understand how she could have cast a spell she didn't know how to cast. Now, dancing a dance she had no memory of learning, she thought she understood.

The dance lesson had 13 students, all of them in white or silver. Elle and Kae were there, moving with fluid grace through the elaborate steps. Their tessili sat in line on the stones with Phril.

Increasingly, over the course of the hour, it was the holdstones that preoccupied Jey. They were unremarkable at a glance. Dull and gray, smooth all over, they varied in size and shape. But they were all the right size for a tessila to settle onto and relax. It seemed to Jey, based on the undercurrent of Phril's thoughts, that they were also warm.

And, Jey was beginning to suspect, Phril's presence on one of those stones enabled her to remember how to dance.

As she let herself be swept through the turns again and again, listening to the soft rustle of the skirts of her classmates and the repetitive drone of the single orderly playing his violin at the top of the hall, Jey felt as she was in color and everyone else in the room was a pale shade. Every time Professor Tucram's glittering eyes swept over her she felt certain he would stop, do a double-take, and call a halt so he could accuse her of remembering.

But that did not happen. Jey danced until the violin stopped. The couples swayed to a halt. Orderlies bowed. Jey curtsied in time with the other girls. Silence fell on the hall.

Professor Tucram's cane made a brisk tapping on the stone floor as he turned on his heel and headed for the door. "Class dismissed. Collect your tessili."

Jey stood for a moment as the orderly who had been her partner turned from her and began to move with the others towards the door, checking his timepiece with an expression of mild worry. Although they'd spent nearly an hour in close proximity, he didn't say anything to her as he left – no parting words, no comment on what they had or had not accomplished. The orderlies flowed out of the hall. The girls drifted towards the table where their tessili sat curled on the holdstones. Soon, the only orderlies left in the room were the two observers. They were packing up their notebooks and inkpots, speaking to one another in low tones.

Jey followed the tide of silver and white dresses, letting the other girls get ahead of her. The girls were quiet, not speaking as they filed up to the holdstones and encouraged their tessili to step back onto their hands. Most of the tessili seemed reluctant to come. Some needed to be stroked on their jaws or coaxed with wheedling words.

Jey approached Phril. He regarded her with his sharp, bright eye. She expected him to be one of those who resisted leaving his stone, but he was not. He stepped onto her hand the instant she presented it. He did this as the two orderlies who had observed the dance class walked by. She noticed one of them witness the ease with which she collected her tessila. He paused to look at her, brow furrowed. She pretended not to notice him. He moved forward again a moment later, taking a few quick steps to catch up with his companion.

Jey let out a short sigh of relief. Around her, the other girls had collected their tessili. They moved in a vague stream towards the doors that opened onto the quad.

Later, Jey would never quite understand what made her do it. It wasn't something she decided. It was simply something she did. As she turned from the table, she noticed no one was watching her. In an instant, she let her hand trail over the last holdstone on the line. With a smooth, slow movement, she curled her fingers around the small, warm rock. She tucked it into her palm and left the hall.

◈

Five minutes later, Jey almost ruined everything. She arrived at Professor Liam's classroom a minute or two early for her next class, having tucked the holdstone into a broken brillbane husk on her way through the quad. It was the best she could manage. Her white dress had no pockets, no folds, no hidden compartments. It was plain and smooth, with skirts that fell softly past her legs. She wore a soft under shift as well as a pair of silk skivvies. The holdstone was too heavy to stay put in any of her clothing.

She had thought of tucking it into her slipper. But her footwear was soft and delicate as well. She was afraid it would shift and click when she walked.

Hiding it in a husk had seemed her only option. She'd paused, reaching into the pod to pry free a seed sack. As the sack fell into her hand, she tucked the holdstone back into the husk, behind the other pods. Then, she'd given the seed sack to Phril.

It wasn't a perfect hiding place. Other girls might see the broken husk and stop to provide their tessili with a snack. But Jey hadn't had time to come up with anything safer.

Now she walked into Professor Liam's classroom, feeling a slight lessening of the tension that had been riding her shoulders all day. She wasn't sure why, but she liked Professor Liam. And he, after all, had told her to cast the spell on Phril. Walking into Liam's classroom the day before was the first thing she could remember – the beginning of the path that started out of thin air.

That couldn't be a coincidence, Jey was sure. So she walked into the classroom again today with a hopeful sense she might learn more.

Later, it would eat at her, how close a thing it had been. She strode into the room with too much purpose, too much knowledge on her face. But it was that first, small mistake that saved her from a worse one.

Professor Liam was at the top of the room, leaning against his desk. The two observation orderlies were in the corner, like always. As the door behind Jey fell closed, Professor Liam asked the question she'd been anticipating all day. "Ah, Jey. Good morning. Tell me, how is our little experiment progressing?"

Jey almost told him. The words were there, in her head, ready to speak.

It was his face that warned her. After he asked the question, he seemed to see she would answer him. His eyes widened in sudden surprise. Then, his hand, which was resting on the edge of the desk next to him, made a sudden, quick flick to the side. It was the hand that was on the opposite side of his body from the orderlies at their desk.

Jey didn't know what the gesture meant, but she caught the words she'd been going to say. A wave of fear-filled uncertainty washed over her.

Heart pounding, Jey forced the muscles in her face to go slack. She let her head tip to one side. She stared at Professor Liam without saying anything. She'd observed other girls do this, when asked a question they did not know an answer to. They didn't come up with guesses, they didn't answer back. They only stared, as if the words had not been words at all, but some unintelligible, vaguely unpleasant sound.

Professor Liam drew in a quick, shallow breath. "Jey," he prodded, "you remember our lesson from yesterday, don't you?"

Jey let her brows draw together. She turned to stare out the window. In doing so, she noticed the orderlies. Where usually the observers sat in attitudes of studied boredom, these two today carried a different air. They both sat straight at their polished table, staring at Jey with bright, focused eyes. Though they both wore tan robes, one had purple piping along the collar and seams. *High Orderly Fras.* Jey recognized the man, but she had no idea when she'd ever seen him before.

Professor Liam went on. "Professor Straph said you were distracted while sparring yesterday. He said you attributed that to me."

Jey, feeling she'd been silent too long, said, "Yesterday." She let the word come out in a slow, wondering tone, as this was a concept she'd encountered before but did not understand.

"Enough, Liam, you've made your point. See what she knows with help from the holdstone." This came from the High Orderly. He looked annoyed, as if Liam had said something insulting.

Professor Liam gestured to a desk with a holdstone set on its corner. Jey moved forward in slow but easy obedience. Phril was perched on her shoulder, gnawing at the brillbane seed sack. She lifted her hand to him. He stepped onto it willingly enough, holding his seed in his mouth. She then moved her hand so he could step from her skin to the warm stone. He did so without hesitation, crouching again once he was in place so he could continue to work on his sack. Jey settled into her seat.

The room was huge and silent. Sun spilled through the high windows. Jey had to fight the urge to look at the dim corner where the High Orderly sat. "Now," Professor Liam said, "Tell me, how is our little experiment progressing?"

Jey let her eyes slide halfway closed. She felt a strange stirring in her mind, a sense of large shapes moving in darkness. She could feel so many intent eyes upon her. "I …" she faltered. This was much harder than feigning pure ignorance. Clearly, they expected her to know more now that Phril was on the stone. But how much more? "I lost the spell," she finally said after a long pause. She let the words trail out of her one by one. "Some time. After I left. I'm not sure."

Professor Liam looked disappointed, but High Orderly Fras rose to his feet as if satisfied. He was a large man, tall, with a round barrel of a chest and soft, smooth cheeks. As he swept towards the door, he spoke. "No more unorthodox experiments, Liam. Particularly not on this one."

◈

Elle's hair was dark and silky. The other girl rested against Jey's legs in languid peace as Jey leaned against the arm of the couch. On the other side of the large room, Kae stood in front of an easel, holding a brush and palette. Around the outside of the round space with the flashnode at its peak, ten alcoves indented into the exterior wall. Jey had counted them when she and her roommates had returned to their dorm after dinner. Only three of them held beds and small tables. The other seven were full of potted brillbane.

Elle was humming as Jey brushed her hair. While the other two girls seemed easy and content, Jey was boiling with frustration. She'd tried to ask her two friends about what they'd done today. While they'd both answered easily in vague terms, when she pressed she couldn't get them to tell her anything specific. For instance, the question, "What did you think of the new dance?" got her nothing but long silences and troubled frowns. And worse, every time the flashnode went off it reset her friends, completely erasing their memories of the conversation they'd been having.

For the moment, Jey had stopped trying. Both Elle and Kae had seemed to be growing a little agitated. It had seemed the flashnode was going off with increasing frequency. Jey had stopped asking questions. Her friends had lapsed straight back into quiet contentment.

Jey hadn't managed to retrieve the holdstone until after dinner, and she'd done so at some risk. She'd drifted towards Professor Liam's classroom, pretending to follow Phril with mild irritation as he'd gone for the broken husk again in search of another seed sack. Other girls had drifted around her as they headed to their dorms for the night. She'd felt exposed and conspicuous, walking on a line different from the others.

But she'd retrieved the holdstone, tucked it into her palm, and given Phril another seed. She'd made her slow, quiet way back to her dorm. She'd tucked the holdstone into a small notch in the wall. It was behind her bedframe – a place where one of the stones of the wall had crumbled away to form a small pocket large enough to hold a few small items.

Now, as Jey brushed her friend's hair and listened to the low tone of her humming, her heart began to pound as she considered what she knew. Her memories started with that day in Professor Liam's classroom – the day he'd asked her to cast a passive shield on Phril. Since then, Jey could remember.

Elle's purple tessila was stretched out on the girl's thumb, wings drooping in content relaxation. Jey experienced a strange feeling of déjà vu as she looked at him, convinced she'd lived this scene before. Not once, but many times.

Phril was perched on a brillbane stalk in the corner, gnawing on his seed with furious enjoyment. Jey sent him a mental nudge, a suggestion to make his way beneath her bed and climb into the crevice where the stolen holdstone lay.

He went with some reluctance, carrying his seed in his mouth and glaring at her. When he was settled, Jey tried to relax. She set the brush down and began to braid the long, fine strands of Elle's hair. Jey imagined Professor Liam's deep, gentle voice saying, "Cast a passive shield on Elle's tessila." Jey had gotten so used to holding Phril's passive shield she almost forgot she was doing it at times. And now, with Phril on the holdstone, she found it was easy to weave another spell just like it. She summoned several strands of magic, knit them together with the proper weave, and snugged the spell over Elle's tessila.

The diminutive purple creature sat up with a sudden start. Like Phril, Elle's tessila had liquid black eyes set into a narrow face. Unlike Phril, Elle's tessila had a set of spikes that formed a sharp fan around the back of the skull. Now, although the animal was small enough to perch on her friend's thumb, Jey felt a sudden shock of fear as Elle's tessila fixed its sharp eye on her and let out a fierce, angry hiss.

Jey's hands forgot about the braid. She concentrated. She could feel the tessila was resisting her desire to secure the spell into place.

Elle opened her eyes. She looked down at her hand. Jey couldn't see her face, but she could imagine the small frown creasing her forehead. She moved her other hand, bringing it in to stroke her tessila along the jaw. She said, "Quiet down now, love. Everything is all right."

Elle, unaware of what Jey was doing, could only have meant to sooth in general. But the tessila seemed to apply the words to the situation at hand. Still glaring at Jey, the tessila quieted. Jey felt the animal stop resisting the spell. Hurrying so as not to let her moment pass, Jey finished the weaving, snugged the spell into place, and let go.

The tessila settled back down on Elle's thumb, broadcasting a mild, disgruntled air. Jey returned her attention to the braid. She suggested to Phril that he could leave the holdstone, if he wanted. He emerged from beneath the bed a moment later, a darting red arrow returning to his perch on the brillbane bush.

Jey tied off the braid with a golden ribbon. She leaned down to say, very softy, next to Elle's ear, "Elle, I need to explain some things. I think, from now on, you're going to be able to remember."

CHAPTER 4

Jey had just finished her explanation when the door to their room opened. She was unable to prevent herself from jumping at the harsh click of the latch and the way the door swung in with enough force to bang against the wall.

Fortunately, both Elle and Kae startled too. Elle sat up in a quick jerk to gaze towards the door with wide eyes. Kae froze in the act of reaching brush to canvas. Her tessila, which had been flying lazy loops around her head, darted down to cling to the shoulder of her dress.

Two men stood in the open door. One of them spoke in a tone of frustrated impotence. "We always enter their rooms quietly, Nylan. Particularly the seniors. Startling them can have consequences."

The speaker was an orderly. Jey recognized him as the one who'd guided her forward after the flashnode had gone off outside the dining hall – the older of the two whose conversation she'd overheard.

Jey hardly registered his words. She recognized the other man, and that name. *Nylan.* She felt a shock in her sternum, accompanied by a frantic desire to run.

But she couldn't run. For one thing, the men were blocking the door. For another, running would give her away.

The orderly was still speaking. "I must insist you wait. There must be at least two orderlies present any time students are with a professor or a handler."

Not heeding the orderly, Nylan stepped into the room. His eyes sought Jey and settled onto her. "As High Handler, that rule does not apply to me." His tone was unpleasant and sneering. He strode into the room, filling the space with violent, bristling energy.

He strode straight to Jey, who jumped back from his approach, cringing and flinching in spite of herself. The orderly came in as well, trailing behind in ineffectual persistence. His voice was higher and smoother, but no less angry. "Perhaps not in the deployment blocks, but you have no such clearance here."

Nylan appeared not to hear. He followed Jey as she backed away, pressing forward until she bumped into the stone wall between two alcoves and could retreat no further.

Phril, agitated, leapt from his perch on the brillbane bush. He flashed through air, darting for Nylan's eyes like an angry spark. Nylan raised a hand as if to dash the tessila to the ground.

The orderly shouted. "No!" His voice was high and panicked. Nylan seemed to realize what he was doing. He only used his hand to shield his face. Phril dashed himself against the man's fingers, clawing with his tiny talons, hissing and snarling with hot fury.

"Contain your creature, girl." Nylan grated these words from between clenched teeth.

"Here," Jey whispered, tapping her shoulder, remembering at the last instant not to call her tessila by name. But Phril was angry. She could feel his rage. He wanted to tear Nylan to pieces, wanted to destroy him as completely as he'd shredded the seed sack earlier. In other circumstances, it might have been funny. The tessila wasn't even as long as Nylan's nose.

But nothing about this moment was amusing. Jey could sense the potential for disaster. It hung in the air like a silent promise. Jey sent Phril a sharper command, this one silent.

With evident reluctance, the tiny creature left off attacking Nylan's face. The orderly had caught up by then and had set a hand on Nylan's shoulder as if to push him away from Jey. He was spluttering half sentences. "Irreversible damage … no authorization."

Nylan lowered his hand as Phril settled. Ignoring the orderly, he reached out and seized Jey's right wrist. He pushed the sleeve of her dress up her arm to reveal the strange gash. It was less red now, perhaps a little smaller. But it still gave off that faint blue tinge around the edges.

Nylan dropped the arm as quickly as he'd seized it. He let the orderly force him back a few steps. His face was dark, eyes sharp with anger. "Why didn't you tell me?" He snapped the words in a tone so harsh, Jey flinched.

Jey's heart was pounding. Phril's violent anger was like a red haze clouding her vision. Fortunately, she had no idea what he was talking about. The blank look she directed at him was genuine. Of course, she'd been aware of the mark on her arm. The orderly that helped them to bed each night had rubbed ointment on it yesterday. She also remembered Professor Liam commenting on it. And it pained her, sometimes, if she pressed up against something or bumped into that place.

But she didn't know where it had come from any more than she knew anything else from before the day Professor Liam had told her to cast a spell on Phril and leave it there.

"She can't answer you without a holdstone, you idiot." The orderly was fully red in the face now. He kept glancing towards the door as if expecting reinforcements.

Nylan reached into his vest and pulled out a syringe. Jey saw it, and her heart leapt. She felt a sudden fierce anticipation, a feeling of desire so intense it churned in her veins like fire.

The orderly saw it too. His red face paled, his eyes widening with horror. "Not here, Nylan. Great Trisis, man. Are you mad?"

Nylan held out one rough-palmed hand. He locked his angry gaze onto Jey's. She couldn't look away. "Give me your tessila," he said.

The orderly pushed himself in front of Jey, shielding her with his soft body. "No. Absolutely not. This is insanity. You'll bring it all down upon our heads."

Phril, in any case, had tucked himself into the warm hair at the base of Jey's skull, quivering with fear and anger. She knew he wouldn't have gone, even if she'd told him to.

The two men faced each other for what seemed an age. Behind them, Jey could hear the quiet sound of Elle crying.

Then, at last, six more orderlies burst through the door, robes flapping, puffing as if they'd sprinted all the way across the quad. Perhaps they had.

Nylan knew he was beaten. With a quiet oath, he stepped backwards, returning the syringe to his vest. As the six orderlies hurried across the stone floor, sandals slapping, all of them asking questions at once, he turned and stalked back across the room.

As he left, he spoke. "Perhaps they'd be more effective if you didn't coddle them so much."

With that, he was gone, leaving the door flung open behind him.

◈

Nylan stalked into the audience hall – a spacious, round room that overlooked the quad. It was a room Nylan was familiar with. Once a week, he was summoned here to report outcomes.

Today's meeting, however, was not routine. It was barely dawn. Nylan had been shaken out of his bed as the first light had begun to pale the horizon. He'd been alarmed at first, certain one of the girls had finally snapped, that something had gone terribly wrong.

But no. It was nothing so dire. Nylan had merely angered the bureaucrats with his unorthodox behavior the day before. And today he would have to face the consequences.

Nylan wasn't sure what the orderlies used this hall for. It had seating for a great many – more orderlies, he suspected, than currently resided at the academy. But that was not surprising. There was space for more professors, more handlers, more students.

Which was one of the reasons Nylan was constantly stressed these days. It was growing increasingly difficult to meet the demands placed upon him. While the number of students at Tessili Academy was falling, the number of opportunities Nylan was expected to complete was not.

It was a real problem, and one that showed no indication of going away. If Nylan hadn't had so much at stake, he might have found a grim irony in the academy's plight. After all, this outcome was predictable. If you systematically cull a population that expresses certain heritable traits, those traits are going to become scarce as time goes on.

There was no quick fix. Nylan had proposed what he thought a reasonable solution to see it summarily rejected. Alarmingly, the idea of keeping the girls active for one more year had gained traction not long ago, almost to the point of being enacted. But then this crop of seniors came along. Support for that idea vanished.

But none of that was why Nylan was here today. He knew that. So he strode in, stopped on the circular floor before the large desk where High Orderly Fras and two attendants presided. He fixed the large, soft man with his glittering stare. Behind the orderly, the sky was a pale shade of pink through the high, narrow windows. "You wanted to see me, Fras?"

Nylan's relationship with the High Orderly was not a comfortable one. They existed on two separate trees of power. The High Orderly ran the academy. He oversaw the other orderlies and monitored the students. He was responsible for every decision, small and large, that pertained to the daily life within these walls. His authority on certain matters was total.

He did not, however, have authority over Nylan. Nylan was on a different, separate, ladder. He answered only to the Dean. What's more, as High Handler, he was privy to certain truths the orderlies could only guess at.

Fras knew this, and at times responded to Nylan's very existence as a personal insult. Now, he stared back at Nylan. His eyes were hard and flat. He said, "Explain yourself."

Nylan knew what Fras wanted him to explain. His forced entrance into the academy last night had been against protocol. He'd known that at the time. But he'd needed to see — to confirm for himself the rumor that had run to him through the gossip chain of the orderlies was true. And now that he'd seen what he'd seen, it changed everything.

"High Orderly Fras, perhaps you're not aware. One of our students returned from an opportunity with an injury …"

Fras cut him off before he could finish his sentence. "Not just any student, Nylan. Your student. You were handler on the opportunity in question, were you not?"

Nylan looked up at the other man, feeling his gut stir with disgust. He could never quite set aside the visceral feeling of repulsion he experienced whenever he was in close quarters with an orderly. Fras was no exception. This was a caricature of a man – his voice strangely high, the lines of his body too soft, too round. "I was. The injury was not evident when she returned because it was inflicted by magic. The way it emerged is consistent with our research. A deflected spell will leave a mark, but it can take several hours before it becomes visible to the eye."

High Orderly Fras sat up a little straighter in his desk. His soft cheeks quivered with contained irritation. "So you decided to break every access rule we have, barge into the senior dormitory well past faculty hours, and risk unsettling the three most dangerous operatives we have at our disposal?"

It had been a rash thing to do. But Nylan hadn't been able to wait. For one thing, if the wound was magical in nature it could disappear at any time. He'd needed to see for himself, to be certain. And he had seen. Now he must deal with the enormous implications of that one narrow, blue-tinged gash.

"With all due respect, Fras, I seem to be the only one who recognizes the severity of the situation. Do you not understand what the mark means?"

The question hung in the slowly dawning room. Outside, the sky was brighter. The hesitant cheeps of sleepy birds drifted in through the windows. The two orderlies with Fras seemed suddenly very busy with their notes.

Fras stood, leaning forward to place two meaty palms on the desk. "She did it herself, Nylan. She cast her own spell, bungled it, and it hit her arm, leaving the mark."

Nylan began to protest, to explain why this was impossible on several levels, but Fras slapped the table with one enormous hand. The shock of the loud sound surprised Nylan into stillness.

"That is what happened." Fras grated these words out between clenched teeth, annunciating each one as if it was its own sentence. "And as for you, Nylan, if you ever set foot inside my walls without authorization again, my orderlies will shock you senseless before you're two steps past the gates."

◈

Kae drifted out of the dorm room, heading for her first class. She murmured a soft, "See you," over her shoulder, and was gone.

Elle, who was finishing at the wash basin, turned to look at Jey with a plaintive expression. "I don't know how I'm going to do it," she said. Her voice was quivery, her eyes wide.

Jey looked at her friend with a mix of sympathy and worry. Elle, like Jey, could now remember. With Jey's spell knitted into place around her tessila, the flashnodes no longer affected her. Which meant she could remember Nylan's strange intrusion into their room, and everything that had happened this morning. She also, like Jey, retained a general if imprecise understanding of the academy as a whole. But she had no specific memories of anything that had happened before Jey had cast the spell.

Jey had tried to explain everything, but she was afraid she'd done little more than make Elle afraid. The other girl had jumped visibly every time the flashnode had gone off this morning. Afterwards, each time, Kae had gone still and silent, then said something that was either repetitive or apropos of nothing. Elle had seemed to grow more disturbed as the morning had progressed.

Now it was time for them to separate and make their way through the day ahead of them, pretending to be like all the other students.

Jey tried to be reassuring. "It's easy," she said. "Move slowly and look blank any time anyone says something to you. If your tessila is on a holdstone, do answer questions, but pretend it takes you forever to come up with the answer. When in doubt, don't say anything at all."

Outside, they heard the click of the neighboring dorm's door falling shut and the soft step of other students moving past the room. Elle took a deep breath, looked at herself in the mirror, and held out her finger. Her tessila alighted there. "Ok. Right. Easy." She took a step towards the door, then looked back over her shoulder. "Aren't you coming?"

Jey was sitting on the edge of her bed, Phril perched on her shoulder. "You go ahead." She forced a quick smile. "Probably better for us not to be out and about together for now. It would be too easy to make a mistake."

Elle nodded, gave Jey one last, long look, and stepped out the door.

Jey sat a moment longer, staring down at the soft slippers on her feet. Her heart was pounding so hard Phril was getting concerned. She waited several beats, making sure Elle wasn't coming back. Then, she opened her hand.

A syringe lay in her palm. The glass tube was warm with the heat of her skin, the needle bright and sharp in the early light. She stared down at it in a mix of fear and wonder.

She remembered taking it from Nylan. She'd seen him tuck it into his vest and turn for the door. She'd recognized the moment as an opportunity she was unlikely to ever have again. She'd done something, then, something she didn't fully understand. She'd woven a spell. She'd done it without thinking, and it had resulted in Nylan and the orderly going still for two heartbeats. It had been enough time for Jey to lunge forward, snatch the syringe from Nylan's vest, and return to her position behind the orderly. A moment later, she'd tucked the syringe beneath the corner of her mattress.

In the aftermath of Nylan's visit, with the orderlies swarming the place and carrying on, with trying to pretend she'd forgotten what had happened after the flashnode went off, with worrying Elle would give them away, she'd almost convinced herself it hadn't happened.

But when everything had calmed down and she'd crawled, at last, into bed, she'd checked and felt the cold, hard cylinder where she'd left it.

Now, she stared at the small amount of clear liquid inside the tube and tried to decipher what she felt. Last night, the very sight of Nylan had filled her with a sense of deep, abiding hatred. But the syringe had excited her. Until he'd held out his hand. *Give me your tessila.*

Jey squeezed her eyes shut, trying to remember more. She had no time. In a few more minutes she'd be late for class. But if she waited, every hour that passed would increase the chance that Nylan would realize the syringe was missing, that he would connect it to her, that he would come asking questions.

Phril, stressed by her agitation, pressed his small body closer to the warmth of her neck. It was the horror of the thought of him in Nylan's hand that gave her the courage. She rolled up her sleeve, pausing to note the pocked galaxy of pale scars in the crook of her elbow. She took a deep breath, inserted the needle into her arm, and pushed the plunger.

For half a second, nothing happened. Jey removed the syringe and flopped back onto her bed to tuck it into the nook in the wall with the stolen holdstone. She was becoming quiet the little thief, she thought with a wry sense of satisfaction.

Then, as she began to sit up, she felt the change. The drug she'd injected raced through her veins like fire. She had to clench her teeth to contain a scream.

And then, Jey remembered. Jey remembered everything.

◈

"Face your partner, bow. Now orderlies, place your hand. Ladies, touch the shoulder. Good. Begin."

The violin started up. Jey let herself be guided into the first steps of the intricate dance. This time, she did not hesitate. She flowed through the dance in perfect, smooth execution, never missing a beat. Up the row of dancers, she saw Elle stumble. But she didn't look, didn't let her head turn. She kept her face blank, serene, false – the caricature of a pretty doll.

After Jey had injected herself, she'd spent approximately 15 seconds steeped in all-consuming rage. She'd looked around at her familiar dorm room in blind anger, feeling the sharp prickle of magic in her fingertips, knowing, suddenly, she could blast the flashnode to shards of glass. She could rip the door off its hinges, light the quiet garden of the dorm cloister on fire. She could stalk through the academy and murder every orderly, every professor. She could do it before they knew what hit them.

But then what would happen? She'd have two dozen terrified, broken girls on her hands, and nowhere to take them. She was certain the orderlies had a contingency plan – some prescribed action to take in the event a girl somehow did what Jey had done, and remembered.

So, she did what they had trained her to do. She sat up, took a moment to smooth her dress and her face, and went to class.

Now, at least, she had some time to think. Her body knew the dance. The hall was silent except for the rustling of skirts, the pale notes of the violin, and Professor Tucram's low litany of instructions. When Jey had come in today, she'd feared, briefly, there would not be enough holdstones for all the tessili – that her first theft would be revealed in this moment. But there were enough stones on the high table. Which meant there was a good chance the missing stone had been noted. Whether or not anyone suspected her, Jey could not know.

She couldn't know, so she put it out of her mind. She had to focus on what she did know. She whirled through turn after turn. More and more memories surfaced in her mind. Most of them took place at night, riding out across the moonlit road towards the glittering town that lay in the valley below, holding a passive echo spell in place around herself and her horse, so anyone who might be able to see them would not register her presence.

Mostly, she remembered Nylan – his glittering, hard eyes. She remembered the agony of being parted from Phril, the implicit consequences of failure.

And she remembered something else, too.

Graduation.

Just thinking that word was enough to cause the blind rage to try to rise again. She pushed it aside. Anger would not help her right now.

Graduation happened every fall. Every fall, the seniors walked across a small stage, shook the dean's hand, and received a diploma.

And every fall, Jey now knew, the seniors died.

"L134, eyes straight ahead. No craning about like that." Jey heard Professor Tucram speak her friend's number. She had to fight the urge to look up the row of dancers to check on Elle. Now that she knew everything, now that she could remember, she worried she'd been premature with casting her spell on Elle's tessila. She didn't envy the confusion her friend was now experiencing, the stress of trying to blend in, of feeling conspicuously awake among a group of sleepwalkers.

Jey no longer felt that way. She, after all, had been trained extensively in the art of deception. She'd spent hours learning how to read a room, to asses threat levels, to infiltrate her target and carry out her mission. She was a weapon – the culmination of 13 years of careful crafting.

Now, she wondered if it might be kinder to pull the spell off Elle's tessila, to expose her again to the muddling effects of the flashnodes. As the dance took her closer to the top of the hall and the bright row of tessili basking on their holdstones, Jey could feel how easy it would be. One little tug, and her spell would come free.

The dancers whirled, soft shoes whispering. The violin played. Jey was soon two pairs from the top, one pair, none. She reached out for the spell.

Elle's purple tessila occupied a stone towards the far end of the table. As Jey focused, the small creature opened its eyes. They locked onto Jey. The tiny animal seemed to understand what she would do. It deflated, somehow. It closed its eyes again. Where before it had seemed content, now it seemed desolate.

Jey hesitated. The dance moved her on. As she wove her way through the steps, she let the spell settle back into place. She understood, now, that she would not do it. The thought of erasing what Elle had begun to learn felt a little too much like murder. And while Jey had most certainly committed murder before, she'd never done it of her own volition.

◈

Elle, Jey and Kae walked into their rooms together, white skirts swishing, tessili darting in the air around their heads. Jey closed her eyes and took a deep breath as the door latched behind them. They'd made it through the day, at last.

Kae, looking dreamy, wandered towards her easel. She stopped before it and stood considering the half-finished painting there as if she'd never seen it before.

Elle headed straight for the couch and flopped onto the cushions. Now she gazed at Kae with a look of haunted horror. "When are you going to tell Kae? You're going to put the spell on her tessila, too, aren't you?"

Kae's tessila, a bright speck of green in the air, swept up to perch on the edge of the canvas. Jey sighed and took her normal seat on the opposite end of the couch. A hairbrush lay on the table. She seemed to recall an endless stretch of evenings, of brushing out Elle's hair, of weaving it into a braid, of tying the braid off with a golden ribbon.

She shuddered and faced her friend. "Elle," she said, "there's more." Jey herself had managed to avoid using a spritzer all day. She'd seen Elle use one several times. She now suspected it was the effect of the spritzer's drug that

Nylan's shot had eradicated. "Give me your hand," she said.

With a little grimace, Elle sat up. She leaned forward, setting her cool fingers in Jey's.

Jey closed her eyes. She tried not to think overly hard about what she was doing. What she knew about magic was accessible to her now, but also dim, somehow. It was as if those memories were behind a screen of some kind, comprehensible only through use. She could have cast the passive shield spell on Kae's tessila in a heartbeat, but she couldn't have explained to Elle how to do the same.

Now, she tried to feel inside her friend's body, comparing it to what she could feel of herself. Over the course of the day, she'd become increasingly aware of a problem. If the spritzer drug blocked her access to certain memories and Nylan's drug restored those memories, she had a finite amount of time. Tonight, an orderly would come into her bedroom. He'd set his hand on her forehead, watch the rise and fall of her chest. Then he would mist the air above her with the drug that would make her forget.

She couldn't let it happen. The very thought of it made her skin prickle with terror.

Jey spoke to Elle, making her voice low and gentle. "You can make new memories, now, but you're blocked from your old ones. It's because of the spritzer, the drug we inhale several times a day."

Elle nodded. Above them, the flashnode went off. Kae, across the room, went briefly still.

Jey tried to focus more deeply on her friend. "I can't get more syringes. It was only the sheerest dumb luck I ever got one in the first place. Which means, we need another way."

Elle's brow crinkled. Jey could see the tension in her, the fear and confusion. On reflex, Elle reached for the spritzer bottle that sat on the low table next to the couch. Then she froze, grimaced, and let her hand fall back to her lap.

That gave Jey an idea. She reached for the bottle herself and set it in her lap. Then she closed her eyes.

She tried to approach the problem. There was the drug in the bottle, and there was the drug in her friend. The drug affected her friend's ability to remember. She thought about weaving a spell that would be attracted to the drug, that would burn it up like Nylan's shot had done.

Across the room, Kae continued to paint. Jey rose, collecting a saucer from the tea tray. She unscrewed the top of the spritzer and poured a few drops of the drug onto the saucer. Then she closed her eyes, wove a spell, and released.

She felt magic pour from her. She felt it react with the drug. There was a soft glow in the air above the saucer, then the little pool of liquid was gone.

Jey turned to Elle, who was watching her with wide, dark eyes. "I can try to burn the drug out of your veins," she said. "If I succeed, you'll know everything."

Elle looked at Kae, who wasn't showing the faintest curiosity in what they were doing. She gave a tremulous laugh and said, "What if you don't succeed?"

Jey felt her heart give a clench. She lowered herself back into her seat. Around them, the academy was quiet. The orderlies went out of their way, she knew now, to keep it that way, to make the place feel peaceful, serene, and safe.

It was all a horrible lie.

She looked her friend in the eye. "I don't know," she said. As far as she could recall, she'd never tried any magic like this before. It was improvisational. What had worked in a saucer might not work in the human body. But she had no time to come up with anything better. "It could kill you, I suppose."

Elle closed her eyes. Her tessila, purple and small, shoved his way into the curl of her relaxed hand. Elle said, "We're going to die anyway, soon. Aren't we?"

Jey looked at Kae. She was still painting, her face smooth and blank, untroubled. "Yes," Jey said. "We have six months, at the most."

Elle looked down and ran her finger along her tessila's chin. Her eyes were luminous with tears. She said, "Then we have to try."

CHAPTER 5

A storm blew in with nightfall. When an orderly came into their room to close the windows, all three girls were engaged in perfectly normal activities. Kae was painting. Elle had taken up an embroidery hoop. Jey was holding a sketchbook and a pencil. Phril was on the table, posing.

None of the girls reacted when the orderly entered. He moved quickly but smoothly, drawing the windows shut and latching them against the rain that was starting to patter on the panes. As he left, he said over his shoulder, "Almost time for bed, girls."

They all made small, vague noises of assent. Then the door closed.

Kae turned to look at the door, eyes hard. "I can't think why we shouldn't kill them all now." Her voice was low, full of the burning anger Jey felt in her own heart when she thought about all that had been done to her.

Elle tied off a piece of thread. Her voice was mild when she answered. "You don't mean that, Kae. For all we know the orderlies don't know any more than we did."

Jey listened to them talk with a sense of quiet wonder. It had worked. Her clumsy, improvised spell had worked. She'd blasted the drugs out of her two friends. They'd spent the last hour practicing, each taking a deep inhalation of the spritzer mist, then letting the others burn it away. All three of them found the spell quite easy to execute.

Jey had also experimented with blocking the spritzer from affecting her at all, at containing the drug as soon as it entered her system. She wasn't able to get it all on the first go, but it didn't seem to matter. The drug didn't act quickly enough to make her forget how to work the spell before she had the time to cast it several times.

Which meant, Jey was no longer in danger of forgetting.

While her roommates were still struggling to come to terms with their new self-awareness, Jey was experiencing a sense of giddy relief. She wasn't alone anymore. Her friends remembered. She remembered. Between the three of them, she thought, they would find a way out.

Kae was quiet, as if surprised by Elle's comment. She paused, paintbrush held aloft, face thoughtful. "I guess you might have a point, there. What about the professors?"

Elle's face went a little harder. "They have to know," she said. "After all, they're the ones who teach us."

Jey thought of Professor Liam. Increasingly, she wondered about him. She thought back on the moment he'd told her to cast the spell on her tessila and hold it. Had he known what it would do? Had he done it on purpose? Or had it been a thing of pure chance?

Jey looked at the mark on her forearm, the one Nylan had barged in to see last night. It was fading, going light. She remembered, now, what had happened. She'd been told to go to a particular house, to change a lord's mind about an upcoming vote in the House of Laws.

But a man had been waiting there. He'd worn a cloak with the hood pulled up. He'd tried to talk to her when she'd dropped her passive echo spell. She hadn't seen him in the corner of the room – in retrospect, she realized, because he'd been casting a passive echo spell of his own.

She'd attacked him instantly. He'd seemed startled, blocking her incoming knife with a blast of pure magic. She hadn't stopped to think about it at the time. She'd kept at him, whirling in for another strike. He'd blocked that one too, with a staff he summoned out of thin air. He'd seemed about to say something when the lord, who'd been sleeping in the great bed at the top of the room, sat up.

The hooded man had looked her in the eye, and vanished.

Jey decided to say something about Professor Liam to the others. But before she could speak, the latch on their door clicked again. An orderly bustled into the room. He was a small man, with the smooth face and thin limbs all the orderlies seemed to have. He clucked when he saw them. "Time to clean up and get changed, girls. Come on, now. It's bed time."

The girls began to put away their things. Jey had to remind herself to move slowly, to not focus her eyes too sharply on anything in the room. Elle and Kae began to do the same.

The flashnode in the ceiling went off. All three of them froze, going entirely still. Jey held herself that way for a moment. Then she blinked a few times and began to stare at the closed notebook in her hand with what she hoped was a vague expression. Elle and Kae made variations of the same face.

Jey, aware of Elle's blank eyes, felt a sudden, furious desire to laugh. It raced through her body, snagging in her throat like a living thing. She fought it, struggling to keep her face passive, her thoughts smooth.

The orderly heaved a huge sigh, as if he'd been asked to fill a hole he'd only just finished digging. "Bed time girls," he repeated in the same, smooth voice. "Time to clean up and get changed."

Jey, fighting the laugher, turned to look for her night dress.

Then, as the orderly came to help with the buttons on the back of her dress, she wondered when she had last really, truly laughed.

She couldn't remember.

She stood while the orderly's deft hands worked their way down her back, the desire to smile gone.

◆

The next morning dawned fine and fresh. Glittering rainwater dripped from the gray tile roof of the cloister compound. The bright gardens all but glowed in the new sun.

Jey stared out the window as she brushed her hair to braid in preparation for the coming day. She'd slept poorly, jumping at every creak in the eaves and shift in the wind. She'd been so afraid she wouldn't wake when the orderly came in to spritz them, that she would sleep through it and find her mind closed and shuttered again in the morning.

It hadn't happened. She'd heard the orderly enter. She'd blocked the effects of the drug. This morning, she could still remember.

But now she had a new problem. It stood on the other side of the smooth lawn. A wall – gray and solid, glittering with fallen rain, throwing its thick shadow across the ground.

If it had been an ordinary wall, it wouldn't have been any kind of barrier. Jey could think of a half a dozen ways to escape over it, under it, to sneak through the gatehouse, or force her way past the guards.

The problem wasn't the wall. The problem was the magic.

She could barely sense it from this distance – a slow shimmer in the morning light. It permeated the stones of the wall and the ground below and the air above. It was a subtle spell, and it was a targeted one.

As Jey watched, a flock of small brown birds wheeled over the wall to settle in one of the rosebushes that grew at its base. The magic didn't affect them. Had a human climbed over the wall, it wouldn't have touched him either.

The magic in the wall harmed only the tessili.

Jey knew this, because she'd worked on the wall. Once a week, Professor Liam led a group of his most accomplished passive casters out to stroll along the wall's base, to test the shieldstones set in among plain stone blocks. Every week, the students replenished these with their own magic, refilling any that were growing weak. Jey could remember doing it, over and over, year after year, strengthening and caring for the magic that kept Phril prisoner.

Behind her, Elle and Kae seemed to be experiencing similar thoughts. The other two seniors looked tired, as if they too had spent much of the night awake and worrying. Now, Jey thought ahead to the charade that would be her school day. She felt abruptly exhausted.

As if reading Jey's thoughts, Elle sat down on the couch, thin shoulders bowed as if beneath a great weight. "I can't do it," she said in a strained voice. "How long will we have to keep pretending?"

Kae straightened from securing her slipper. Her tone was sharp and determined. "We'll keep pretending until we find a way past that cursed wall. Maybe we can figure out a way to sabotage the spell during our maintenance shifts."

Jey looked over at Kae, a little feeling of hope lifting her heavy spirits. "That's a good idea. If all three of us passed over one shieldstone each time we do maintenance, maybe we can make a gap, a place where our tessili could fly through."

Elle was frowning, twirling the end of the braid between her fingers. "But the other students. They'll notice and fix it."

Kae answered quickly, before Jey had a chance to respond. "We could cast a passive echo spell on the stone. Then the other girls will pass over as if it's not there."

All three of them considered this plan in silence for a moment. Phril, who had been rubbing his red scales to a shine against the outside of a brillbane husk, leapt into the air to make a darting loop around the domed ceiling.

Jey could feel he was happy. His scales had been warmed by the morning sun. His wings felt strong and true.

Jey watched him, feeling her heart turn over with that deep sense of love. She imagined him flying over the wall, of following her out of this place, to freedom. "It might work."

Elle was staring down at the bright rug under the table. "What about the other girls? We can't leave them."

Kae's response was immediate and fierce. "We *can* leave them, Elle. We can, and we will. It's going to be hard enough for the three of us to avoid calling attention to ourselves as it is."

Elle went quiet, staring ahead in silent sadness.

Jey spoke. "We'll come back, Elle. The others, they have more time. Our leaving won't harm them. Once we're free we can come up with a plan to bring this place down from the outside."

◈

Orderly Brint had come to terms with the reality of his situation. In many ways, he recognized what he had was better than the life he most likely would have ended up with had the course of events taken his life in another direction.

When he'd been sentenced to death for poaching, Brint had thought he would die. He'd thought he would die, and dying had seemed like a relief. It meant no more scrounging for food, no more losing people he loved. He'd been only a boy then, not quite shaving. He'd had a boy's perception of the world.

They'd come to him the night before he was scheduled to hang. They'd made him an offer. Death, or castration. Removal from the earth, or removal from society. If he chose to let him do their surgery, he would be safe forever. They promised him food and shelter and an easy life. They'd brought him food, even, when they'd come to him – a loaf of bread and a wheel of cheese. They'd spoken to him while he ate.

It hadn't been a hard decision for a boy who'd been hungry his whole life to make.

As far as Brint's parents knew, their son was dead. As far as the world knew, the place where he now passed his days did not exist. He'd undergone his surgery. The years had passed. The marks of manhood that had begun to appear had faded from Brint's body. His muscles had softened. His cheeks were as smooth as a girl's. He lived here, a prisoner kept in peace and plenty. There was a rhythm to his days. He had purpose. He had security. Did he need freedom as well?

Not all the orderlies saw it that way. Some endlessly plotted their escape. Some chafed and snarled and scowled until they were reprimanded. Sometimes, the reprimand made no difference.

When an orderly was removed for misconduct, the others were always informed. High Orderly Fras would call them to convene in the evening hours, after the girls had been put to bed in their dorms. He would always explain the infraction, the series of steps that had been taken to correct the wayward orderly's behavior. He would speak with regret about being forced to come to the decision to remove the orderly from the academy. "It's for your safety," he would say, solemn and grim. "It's for the safety of us all."

Fras never precisely spelled out where the orderlies went when this happened, but it wasn't hard to figure out. After all, what could one possibly do with a man who was already dead, but kill him?

Of course, there had been one or two quiet cases – instances where a man had simply disappeared. No reprimands, no noted infractions. Just gone. When this happened, Fras would give the same speech, explaining something had come up suddenly, they'd had to act. Brint wondered, sometimes, if these men had managed to escape.

Brint did not think about escape. He could see no benefit in attempting to return to the outside world. He was now even less likely to scrape out a place for himself beyond the academy walls. What use would the society that had rejected him as a poor boy have for him as a castrated male?

The only thing that bothered him about his life was the girls. The seniors, in particular. He tried not to think about it, tried not to look into their faces, to wonder what was broken in those pretty heads. He didn't believe the girls graduated any more than he believed the orderlies who grew too old to work were retired to a place they could be better cared for in their twilight years. Brint didn't even mind the thought of being quietly murdered in his dotage. If he hadn't been brought to the academy in the first place, his chances of seeing old age would have been too slim to calculate.

In truth, Brint saw little benefit in dwelling on outcomes he could not change. So he did his duty. He did the best he could for the girls. He watched them grow from small, frightened children into vague, scattered teenagers. Then he watched them each receive a diploma. He did not, thankfully, have to watch them die.

He was used to the cycle. But now, the cycle was disturbed.

It had started with the missing holdstone. One evening, the orderlies had been called to the meeting chamber. High Orderly Fras had explained a stone had been lost – most likely bumped off the table in the dance hall and perhaps kicked into a corner or otherwise overlooked. The dance hall had been searched, but the missing holdstone had not been discovered. The next day, Brint had helped search the dormitories. Each chamber had been scoured, the scant belongings allowed to the girls meticulously sorted through and examined.

No holdstone had been found. Brint had been inclined to believe it was merely lost. Holdstones were small. There were any number of ways such things could go missing.

But now there was the more serious matter of the missing syringe. Nylan had called Brint to the deployment block complex the day before. Brint had gone with reluctance, fearing some retribution for the fact that he'd stood up to the High Handler, interfered with him the night he'd swept into the academy flaunting authority he did not have. The guards had caved before Nylan's flat stare and certain step. Not Brint. He knew the rules. He knew, knew for a fact, that handlers were not allowed within the academy walls under any circumstances. A handler most certainly wasn't authorized to go into a dormitory unsupervised and harass a senior.

Brint had responded to the message in spite of his reservations. Nylan had asked him, casually, if he'd happened to hear of anyone finding the syringe Nylan must have dropped in his haste to leave the senior's dormitory that night. Brint had stared at the other man, a feeling of slow unease beginning to uncurl in his belly. He'd said he had not. Nylan had thanked him for coming. Brint had left, unsettled.

And now, today. This morning the orderlies had read the announcement in the small antechamber that lead to their sleeping hall. The seniors, having accomplished so much, would be graduating early. There was to be a special ceremony the following morning. The orderlies were to see the three girls through their day with special care. In the morning, instead of going to class, all students were to convene in the quad after breakfast.

Brint could well guess what would happen after that.

Jey looked up when the orderly came in. It was evening. She and Elle and Kae were enjoying their few hours of solitude before bed time. The three of them had hardly spoken since dinner.

Jey could see the fatigue in her friends' faces. She could feel it in herself. It was exhausting, the charade. More than anything, she feared waking each morning to find one of them gone again, her memory erased by the drug they had to avoid inhaling. Every morning, Jey woke with the fear she'd forgotten something.

And that, perhaps was the hardest thing of all. Jey thought what she knew now was the truth. But what if it wasn't? What if the things she thought were just another version of reality, crafted and placed in her mind for some reason she could not fathom? What if she'd been a different person the day before, or the week before? What if all her memories were false?

There was no use in worrying about such a thing, of course. She had to believe in what she thought she knew, or she would go mad. Still, it was impossible not to wonder. Although Jey now knew more than she had a week ago, there was an awful lot about her situation she did not understand.

The orderly moved through the door, pushing it open with his back and stepping into the room. Jey looked up, noticing with some surprise he was carrying three slim vases, each filled with a delicate floral arrangement. He carried them tucked up against his narrow chest.

Jey resisted the urge to rise and help him. She recognized this orderly. It was the one she'd first recognized outside the dining hall, who'd later pushed himself between her and Nylan when the handler had barged into the senior's dorm. She looked at him now. He was not a young man, and yet he looked nothing like Nylan. Where Nylan had a bristling beard, this man had only smooth cheeks. Where Nylan was all rough hands and square shoulders, this man was soft and slight.

Jey didn't understand, but she felt a quiet affection for this orderly. He was familiar to her, as if she'd once known him well. *He was yours, long ago. Back when you were still a little girl, and you had your own orderly, all to yourself. His name is Brint.*

The thought swirled through her mind like smoke. Jey strained to remember more, but it was useless. Even without the drugs her memory was fragmented, vague, and incomplete. Her clearest recollections were of the opportunities she'd been sent on. Which were the things she least wanted to remember.

The orderly crossed the room to set the three vases on the low table. The glass bottoms clicked as they met solid wood. The orderly straightened, smiled, and looked at Jey. She regarded him with what she hoped was a vacant stare. "These are for you to bring with you in the morning. Tomorrow." He said the words in a casual tone. As he spoke, he began to move about the room, tidying the few stray items that were out of place.

Elle and Kae were watching the man too, now. "Tomorrow?" Kae said. Her voice was bland and distant.

"Yes." The orderly set an empty tea cup back on the rack near the door. It would be removed in the night for cleaning. "For your graduation. The three of you must have distinguished yourselves tremendously. It's been ten years since the last senior graduated early. And then, it was only one."

Jey felt as if her heart stopped beating. In their poses of fake occupation, Kae and Elle went still. It was all Jey could do not to turn and stare at the orderly, to ask him questions, to beg for his help. Tomorrow? They were to graduate tomorrow?

Above them, the flashnode went off.

All three girls took the opportunity to go stiff, to let their eyes unfocus, to blink and go slack.

The orderly, watching them, sighed. His voice was different when he spoke next – hollow, somehow. "Not that my warning will do you any good."

He turned as if to go.

Jey was visited by a sudden memory. It was as clear and bright as the sunset outside the window. In the memory she was a child, running across the quad. She tripped on her skirts and fell onto the stone path. She sat up, palms stinging, and examined the raw red scape on her knee. She began to cry.

Orderly Brint came to her. He snugged her into his soft arms. He kissed her forehead. He took her to the washroom and dabbed a warm, damp cloth on her knee.

Jey made a decision on the spur of the moment. It was a twofold risk, and it was not her life alone she gambled with. But it seemed their only hope.

She turned and spoke. "Brint."

The orderly froze at the sound of his name. He turned, eyes wide with disbelief. She could see Elle and Kae struggling not to react, to retain their passive, blank appearance. Jey continued. "Does Liam know?"

Brint blinked several times, looking confused. "The professor?" he said.

Beginning to fear she'd made a mistake, she let her head drift to the side, to contemplate the middle distance. She said, tone vague, "He's always been my favorite."

◈

The door shut behind Orderly Brint. Outside, the sound of his departing footsteps faded. The three girls sat, listening, until the sound was gone.

Three heartbeats after all was still, Kae turned on Jey. "Have you lost your mind?" Kae's eye were bright with anger. Her words came in a furious hiss.

Jey looked away, shrugging. Orderly Brint had not seemed to take her comment very seriously. He'd looked at her a moment longer, then given a little shake of his head and said, "I see."

With that, he'd left. Now, Jey felt cold and sick with disappointment. She'd been convinced he'd come deliberately to warn them, that he would try to find a way to help. Belatedly, Jey remembered the words Orderly Brint himself had spoken outside the dining hall that day a week or two before. *One of these girls is a thousand times more valuable than you are. Get one of them rattled and I promise you they'll have removed you by morning.*

Elle was in her usual spot on the couch. Her tessila sat in her hand, curled in the cup of her palm. "What are we going to do?" Her voice carried the same tired helpless weight Jey felt in her bones.

"We're going to break out." Kae stalked towards the door as she spoke. "At least, I am. If you two don't want to try, that's fine. But I'm not going to sit around staring at the wall like an idiot, waiting for my own execution."

Elle, agitated, sat up. "Not this instant, Kae. It's too dangerous. And keep your voice down."

Kae was halfway to the door now, her face fierce. "What do you mean it's too dangerous?" She snapped the words with withering impatience. "What's wrong with you two? Don't you see? We're trained assassins. We have magic. They can't fight us."

Jey stood as well, taking a step towards Kae. Her heart was pumping with alarm but she tried to keep her voice gentle. "And what about the wall, Kae? How do you plan to get past that? Even if we murder everyone in this place, we can't leave. We'll have two dozen little girls to care for. We might all starve before we find a way to disable a shieldstone."

Kae frowned, bristling with anger and impatience. "Well what do you propose, then, if you're so smart?"

Before Jey could answer, they heard footsteps outside. Kae's eyes widened. She hurried back to her easel. Jey sat back down on the couch and tried to compose her expression as her heart leapt with sudden, piercing hope. Was it Professor Liam, perhaps? Coming to lead them out?

The door swung open and an orderly walked in. Jey recognized him with surprise. It was the young, muscular orderly Brint had been speaking to by the dining hall. She'd seen him around the quad since then, but she didn't recall him ever coming into their room.

He stopped inside the room. "Come on, girls," he said as his eyes raked over them. There was something unpleasant in his gaze. "Bed time."

Jey tried not to let her confusion show. It was too early for bed, and something about his tone made the hair on her arms prickle. She forced herself to stand, smooth her dress, and move quietly towards her dressing screen. The orderly followed. He helped her with her buttons. His hands were quick and rough, his breathing audible. Jey felt a sense of relief as he walked off to help Elle.

Jey was into her night dress by the time the orderly stepped behind Kae's screen. She heard him say something, heard Kae respond. Her sense of relief vanishing, Jey stepped out from behind her screen to look across the room.

What she saw made her go still. She couldn't see Kae, because she was behind her screen. But the discarded pool of her white dress lay on the floor. The orderly was also partially behind the screen. As she watched, he dropped Kae's night dress to the floor, also.

"Get in bed." The orderly's voice was low and gruff. When Kae hesitated, the orderly repeated his command, giving her bare shoulder a little shove.

With one hopeless, confused look at Jey, Kae complied. Her naked skin was luminous and pale in the wan light. The orderly stopped her as she tried to pull up her light summer quilt. He stood over her, a cruel little smile dancing on his lips. "Just because they've unmanned me doesn't mean I can't still get the job done." His voice was a hard sneer now. "You won't remember in the morning, anyway, and you'll be dead before anyone has a chance of figuring it out." The orderly unbuckled his belt and let it fall to the floor.

Jey stood in stunned silence, a vague sense of terror beginning to snake through her veins. She had no idea what the orderly was talking about but she felt an intense need to defend her friend.

Jey took a step forward. The orderly glanced over his shoulder, looking first at Jey, then Elle, who also stood in her night dress, looking on with quiet worry. "You two stay back," he said. "Or I'll make this harder on your friend than it has to be."

He flung open his robe, turned around and lowered himself down on top of Kae.

For one stunned instant, all three girls were still. Then, Kae exploded. She gave a short shriek of rage that was no less terrifying for being quiet. There was a quick scramble on the bed – limbs tangling, hands groping. Jey had taken two more steps forward when there was a grunt, a flash of blue light, and a crunch.

For a second, all was quiet. Then, with a little snarl, Kae heaved the orderly's body off of her. It fell to the floor with a slack thud.

Jey stared down in silent horror. She could tell by the angle of the man's head that his neck was broken.

◈

"Kae." Elle's voice was a horrified whisper. "You killed him."

Kae left her bed. She stood, naked, over the dead man. She looked down at his bare chest and body, face contorted into a mask of anger. "He was going to …" She trailed off without finishing her sentence then kicked the dead man in the ribs with her bare foot.

Elle averted her eyes, turning her imploring gaze on Jey. "We have to figure out how to hide him." She said this as if Jey possessed the miraculous talent of making dead bodies disappear.

Jey glanced around the dorm. There was nowhere to conceal a body. The room was open, the entrances to the alcoves wide and unobstructed. There were no nooks or crannies, no concealed spaces. The best they'd be able to do would be to drag him behind a changing screen and hope no one thought to come looking for him here.

"I don't know about you two," Kae said, picking up the night dress the orderly had dropped and shrugging into it, "but I'm leaving."

Jey felt as if this was all happening too quickly. Her mind felt numb with confusion and anxiety. She couldn't tear her eyes from the blank look of surprise in the dead man's eyes.

"You can't, Kae," Elle said. "They'll catch you before you're halfway to the wall. And even if they don't, you can't get your tessila past the spell."

Kae gave a derisive snort. She picked up one of her slippers, stared down at it critically for a moment, then tossed it aside. Her tessila was a streak of agitated green, zipping around her head in fast loops. "I'll cast a passive echo spell to hide myself. I'll figure out the rest out as I go." She began to walk, barefoot towards the door.

Jey, stirred to action, moved to block her friend's departure. "How long can you hold a passive echo spell of that size, Kae? Because I can only manage mine for five minutes easily, ten at most."

Kae stopped, scowling. Elle spoke from behind them. "Me too," she said. "Maybe eight minutes if I'm fresh. Then I need a rest.'"

Kae said nothing. She'd stopped walking, but her face was a mask of anger.

"Ten minutes," Jey repeated. "That's how much time we'll have once we leave this room. We need a plan, Kae."

Something in Kae's face crumbled. Her nostrils flared. Jey realized her friend was fighting back tears. Kae glanced over her shoulder at the dead man on the floor.

She shuddered. "If we don't try something, he's right. We'll be dead by this time tomorrow."

Elle strode forward, her body language decisive. She walked to the orderly. With a couple stabs of magic and a swipe of her arm, she ripped a square of fabric out of his robe. She strode to one of the brillbane bushes that stood in a pot by the window. With a few deft movements, she broke all the ripened husks free of their stems, set them in the center of the square of fabric, and tied the edges together to form a tidy bundle. "We'll hide," she said. "We'll find somewhere no one will think to look. We'll take turns with passive echo spells whenever anyone comes near. Then we'll wait, and we'll watch until we figure out a way to get past the wall."

Elle straightened, tossing her long braid over her shoulder. Her tessila darted through the air and landed on the bundle, clinging to the fabric as it swayed in Elle's hand.

Jey looked from one friend to the other. She took a deep breath, let it out, and spoke. "Ok. Yes. That sounds like the best we can do for now."

Behind them, the latch on the door clicked.

CHAPTER 6

If Jey hadn't blocked the spell, it would have killed Professor Liam as he poked his head through the door. Kae sent it off in a spasm of fear and anger. Jey felt it shoot into the air – an active strike spell. She swiped it off its course with her own counter-magic.

Behind them, she heard Professor Liam draw in a quick, sharp breath. Jey hadn't known, for sure, it would be him when she'd blocked Kae's spell. She only knew killing more people was not going to make their escape any easier.

When she saw it was Liam, a red haze bloomed at the edges of her vision. "Kae, you idiot," she snapped. "He's on our side." Jey wasn't sure how she knew this, but she was more certain she could rely on Professor Liam than she was of her own name.

His face a little pale, the professor stepped into the room. Kae's face had gone pale as well at the sight of him. "Sorry," she mumbled.

Liam closed the door behind him and stood for a moment, staring at the three girls in their night dresses and the dead man on the floor. The orderly's robe was unbelted, his chest, legs, and everything between them exposed. The professor swore quietly and strode across the room. He dragged the quilt off Kae's bed and tossed it over the dead man.

He straightened, turning back around. He looked at the girls. His short hair was light brown, shot with gray. His eyes were somber and sad, but also alight with some brilliant curiosity. "All three of you?" he said. "You're all three …" he paused, looking for a word, "… aware?"

Jey nodded. To her amazement, he laughed. "Finally," he said. He stood a moment, shaking his head and chuckling as if he'd heard some wonderful joke. He looked at Jey, eyes intent. "You remember how to get out?" He asked the question as if he was certain she would.

Jey frowned. Her mind stirred, a memory trying to surface. She seemed to recall standing by the wall with Liam. While the other students recharged the shieldstones, she was doing something else – chipping away at one narrow crevice, targeting a fissure in the wall behind a rose bush, making it deeper and deeper and deeper. The work, she suddenly remembered, had been started before her. Liam had only shown her how to continue what was already begun.

She struggled to remember more, but the knowledge faded. She stared at Professor Liam, heart pounding with fear. "I haven't had any spritzer," she said. "Why can't I remember?"

Professor Liam walked across the room and set a gentle hand on her arm. The smile had faded from his face. "It's all right, Jey. Calm down. What they've done to you, year after year after year, it's not as simple to fix as getting rid of the drugs. It's going to take time. It's probable you'll never have complete memories of what happened here. Most likely, that's for the best." His eyes strayed again towards the shape of the orderly beneath the quilt, his expression troubled.

Jey allowed herself to be soothed by his words. She drew in a long, slow breath and let it out again, centering herself as Professor Straph had taught her.

Liam continued to speak. "It's a crack in the wall, down past the stable, in the lower southeast corner. I'll take you."

Kae, who'd recovered from her momentary embarrassment, turned to regard Liam with a look of withering scorn. "A crack in the wall won't do us any good. If it was that simple, our tessili could just fly over."

That little smile returned to Liam's lips. He shook his head. "Not just a crack. Jey here has been working on it for almost a year now, when we could manage it, of course. It's lined in shieldstone, like that which holds the magic of the wall in place."

Kae's expression shifted. She glanced towards the door with a kind of fierce hunger. "Then it's a tunnel," she said. "A tiny tunnel through the magic? Our tessili can pass through safely?"

Liam nodded. Kae took a step towards the door, which Jey was still blocking. "Professor Liam," Jey said. "Thank you. Thank you for coming to us, for making me remember. I know where it is now." It was true. When he'd described the tunnel, she'd remembered as surely as if he'd shown her a map. "You should go back to your rooms."

For a moment, Liam looked as if he might protest. Then he glanced again at the humped shape of the dead orderly. He gave a small, decisive nod. "This evidence will give an explanation for your flight. With any luck, no suspicion will fall on me. I'll stay behind. I'll do what I can do for next year's seniors."

As Kae and Elle began to move towards the door, Jey realized with a sudden strange pang that she might never see this man again. It was overly optimistic, she knew, to think his movements tonight would go unnoticed. She didn't know how he'd gotten himself into the dorm cloister after faculty hours. There was so much she didn't know, so many things she was certain she'd forgotten.

Jey felt a sudden prickling heat behind her eyes. She hurried forward, throwing herself into Liam's arms. He caught her with a startled grimace, then wrapped his arms around her. She could smell the mingled scent of soap and ink.

They stood for a moment. Liam felt warm, solid, and safe. Jey didn't want to let go.

At last, the professor gave her shoulder an awkward pat. "Go now." His voice was quiet. "They'll be onto you soon. And don't forget, the hounds will smell you even with your passive echo spells in place."

Jey nodded, wiping her eyes. She stepped back and turned towards the door as it opened for the third time that evening.

◈

The orderly who was now staring into the room with wide, startled eyes was one Jey recognized. She didn't know his name, but he was one of the regular ones who saw them into bed each night. He was a quiet man, with pale hair and delicate hands.

Now, as Liam took a deft step to the side so the partially open door hid him from view, she watched as the orderly's eyes took in the sight of the three seniors standing in their night dresses, Elle holding a bundle torn out of a robe just like his.

The orderly took two stumbling steps backwards. Before Jey could think of a way to quiet him, to contain the disaster, the man screamed. It was a high wail of sheer terror. Then the orderly turned and bolted, sandals slapping on the stone tiles and echoing through the quiet cloister.

Jey drew in a quick breath as he ran away. Now that the worst had happened, her mind felt suddenly clear and focused. She spoke. "Girls, case your passive echo spells."

She felt the air bend around her. Kae and Elle vanished. She turned to Professor Liam, still standing behind the door. She didn't think he'd been seen, but she couldn't know for sure. She focused, pulling strands of magic into existence in the air around him. She tied off the spell. Liam's eyes widened in surprise as he felt the magic cling to his skin. Then he vanished also.

"I'll not be able to hold it for long, particularly as you get further away," she said. "So hurry."

She felt a soft squeeze on her hand and a brush of air as Professor Liam moved past her and out the door. Jey wove another spell and draped this one around herself. The strain of holding both magics in place made sweat bead on her forehead. She set her jaw. She would hold them as long as she could.

She turned and spoke to the seemingly empty room behind her. "Let's go."

She couldn't see her two friends, not exactly, but she could make out soft spots in the air, places where the landscape seemed to shimmer as if seen through uneven glass. She could hear soft footsteps and feel the whisper of air moving. Mostly, though, she could see their tessili. Phril was all but mad with anxiety now. He darted about her head in frantic loops. "Settle," she told him. She held out her hand and he landed there. She could feel how difficult it was for him to hold still, to allow himself to be restrained. She cupped her hand in a light curl around him, so the spell that concealed her would cover him too.

"Carry your tessili," she whispered to the other two girls, "or they'll give us away."

Around them, the academy was coming alive. Lights flared in dark windows. Doors opened and closed. Orderlies ran everywhere, calling to one another in frantic voices. The three girls left their room and headed to the east. When they reached the corner of the cloister, Jey said, "Up and over. You first Elle."

She could no longer see Elle's purple tessili, but Kae's green one darted and flashed in the air like a frantic spark. She waited in tense silence. In the distance, there was a resonant boom. The orderlies had swung shut the great gates that separated the cloister from the quad. Jey could only hope Professor Liam had gotten out in time.

"I'm up." Elle's voice sounded from above them.

"Go," Kae's voice hissed out of the air beside her. Jey leapt forward.

She had to release Phril to set her hands on the stone pillar. He fluttered to the nape of her neck and hung to the braid there, hissing. She was about to use a little surge of magic to blast a handhold into the smooth stone, but her fingers found one Elle had already made. She focused, bringing tension into her muscles. She climbed.

It was tricky. The holds were shallow and the shouts and slamming doors were distracting. But as she climbed

Jey felt herself slip into a meditative place of stillness where her mind was concerned with nothing but the task of bracing her fingers, molding her feet, pushing herself up the pillar, one step at a time. She could do this. She was prepared. She'd spent 13 years preparing.

Elle was visible when Jey reached the rooftop. She reached out a hand. Jey accepted it. Elle pulled her onto the rough slate tiles of the roof. "Now you, Kae," Jey called down. She too, dropped her passive echo spell to save her strength. As she did she felt the spell that had been clinging to Liam fizzle and fall away. She glanced towards the faculty compound. The building was a dark smudge visible beyond the wall, a few lit windows visible in the night. She couldn't fathom any way he could have arrived safely back in his own rooms by now.

Jey pushed thoughts of Liam from her mind. She and Elle waited on the rooftop, gauging Kae's progress by the darting speck of her tessila. Kae was unwilling or unable to get him to settle.

Jey moved to the other side of the roof, looking out across the smooth lawn that separated them from the wall beyond. It was not a hugely formidable wall. It was thirty feet high, perhaps, and ten feet thick. Without the magic woven into it, the magic that would kill any tessila it touched, it would have been no barrier at all.

Along the top of the wall, torches were being lit. One by one, they flared to life like glaring eyes. Shapes of men in dark uniforms were fanning out from the gatehouse, jogging into position. From the west, she heard excited yips and barks, the clang of a gate being thrown open. She remembered Liam's words. *Remember, the hounds can smell you even with your passive echo spells in place.*

Jey heard a thump. She turned to see Kae now also on the roof. The three of them sat for a moment, watching as the academy swarmed into readiness. Jey found her mouth was dry. A cool breeze stirred her thin night dress, but she was not cold. She felt alive for the first time she could remember.

With a nod to her companions, she leapt off the roof, casting a passive bearing spell to displace her weight and leave it on the rooftop so she fell with less force. She hit the ground and absorbed the impact with her knees. A moment later, Kae and Elle landed on either side of her. Each set down in a ready crouch as Jey had, three fingers against the grass to steady them. They'd all had the same teachers, after all.

The grass was damp and soft beneath Jey's feet. The three girls straightened in unison.

A hound bayed in the darkness. Together, they began to run.

The first hound came barreling out of the darkness, running at speed. It was a tall, fleet creature, with long legs and a narrow head. It was a blur in the night, a flash of white eyes and teeth.

Jey heard Elle give a little shriek as it came towards them. They hadn't recast their passive echo spells yet. They'd thought they would have more time. But the dogs were fast. Far faster than Jey had assumed.

There was a flash and a high yip of pain. Blue light flared in the night. The hound collapsed into a dark heap, dead at Kae's feet.

"Passive echo," Jey hissed. But she knew it was too late. The three girls cast their spells, but there were shouts along the walls as men pointed and cried to one another. That flash of magic had pinpointed their location. The path they'd taken from the academy, straight for the crack in the wall, revealed exactly where they were going. *Stupid, stupid,* Jey thought to herself as she began to run again. She knew Kae was there. Her green tessila was a frantic, darting whir in the air. Elle was not so easy to spot, but Jey could hear her breathing and the soft thump of her bare feet in the grass.

They ran to the wall. More hounds streaked through the darkness around them, but the tall, fast animals were sighthounds. She remembered that lesson suddenly, the knowledge spilling into her brain in a rush. Sighthounds hunted by tracking movement. They were fast and strong and could pull down a deer. But they wouldn't track the girls by scent.

No. The scenthounds would do that.

Behind them, in the darkness, a bay rose up at the base of the outer cloister wall. Jey glanced back and saw the bobbing light of lanterns. More bays joined the first as more hounds picked up the trail. She heard a shouted command and knew they were nearly out of time.

In front of them reared the wall, black and monumental in the night. They reached its base. Jey's eyes searched frantically for the small crack. Terror gripped her heart when she didn't see it immediately. What if she'd come to the wrong place? Or what if it had been discovered and repaired since the last time Liam had been able to bring his class here?

Heart pounding, she stooped behind the rose bush, fingers groping along the rough stone. The hounds bayed again, their voices high and clear, excited and keen.

At last, Jey's fingers found the crack. They snagged on its irregular mouth. Inside, she felt the smooth lining of the shieldstone she'd painstakingly made. It had taken so long. She remembered all the hours she'd spent here, mind focused down to a point, extended deep within the wall. First she had chipped out the passage, then she'd transmuted a thin layer of stone. It had gotten more difficult as she'd gone deeper and deeper into the wall.

But it was finished. She'd completed it in the spring. She could feel the breach in the magic. It was a narrow crack, but it would be enough. She let her breath out with a relief so great it was almost painful.

The hounds were coming. They were visible now, mottled shapes moving across the dark lawn. Jey spoke into the night "Kae, go."

Later, Jey would wonder why she chose to send Kae first. Perhaps it was because Kae had seemed the most decisive, the most angry, the most ready to leave. Perhaps she hadn't had any reason at all. If she'd had time to think about it, she might have realized the one who went first was taking a risk. The tunnel hadn't been tested. They had no way of knowing, for sure, that it was safe to use.

In any case, it was not safe to stay where they were. They had to go. Jey, in that split second, had two names to choose between.

She felt a brief squeeze on her shoulder, saw Kae's tessila dart towards the crack in the wall. There was a shower of stone fragments and the quick sound of Kae's breathing as she scaled the wall. The guards who stood on top stared out towards the lanterns of the group of orderlies who had now reached the dead dog. They had no idea how close they came to death as the lithe, angry Kae passed between them.

Suddenly, there was a hound. It came running down the lawn, nose to ground. It stopped by the rose bush. It raised its muzzle and let out a long, high howl. "Now you," Jey said to Elle. Another brief squeeze on her hand, another darting movement as the purple tessila clawed its way into the crack. And Jey was alone.

◆

It hadn't been difficult for Nylan to figure out where the girls would come over the wall. The guards made it obvious, the way they gathered together, shouting and pointing. Nylan had known better than to think they would let him back into the academy after his little show of temper a few nights before. But he'd be damned if he would see that girl, J114, destroy all he'd worked for. He had given too much. He'd sacrificed his freedom and gone without the most basic comforts and pleasures for years now. He hadn't minded. Not really. He'd had a goal. He'd been making steady progress. Until J114 had come along.

Nylan had already been in a deployment block when the academy had burst into sudden, noisy chaos. He was preparing to send a student on a vital opportunity. It was one he'd intended for J114, but now it was too dangerous to use her. He'd been informed all the seniors were unstable. They'd have their silly graduation ceremony in the morning.

And then, Nylan would kill them.

Which meant tonight he'd had to settle for a greener student – M215, who hadn't developed to the level of proficiency Nylan would have preferred for the night's work. It was, Nylan thought, the great flaw in the way the academy was run. As soon as the girls became effective weapons, they became too dangerous to be allowed to live.

So, Nylan was already worried and frustrated when the academy exploded into frantic activity. No one came to tell him anything, of course. But Nylan wasn't the type who enjoyed being told what to do, anyway. He'd always been independent, quick to act of his own volition.

When he'd realized what must be happening, he'd grabbed a stunrod and strode out of the deployment block. Torches lit the darkness. He walked towards the place of most concentrated activity on the wall. As he walked through the clamoring night, the activity increased. He broke into a jog.

He reached the wall and looked around, suddenly wary. Up on top, all the guards were looking in the other direction, looking inward.

Nylan was no fool. He knew one of these girls could kill him as simply as he could crush the little beasts that gave them all their incredible potential. But he also knew J114 was broken – mind muddled by drugs, fragmented by flashnodes, limited by the strange, artificial life she had led. She would be scared tonight, and perhaps careless. Perhaps it would be possible to take her by surprise.

So Nylan tucked himself into the shadows at the base of the wall. There, he waited.

It was the tessila that gave her away. It appeared suddenly, as if out of thin air. It darted in a frantic loop, a blur of movement in the night. Nylan saw it. He did not hesitate. He didn't know how it had gotten over the wall. It was not relevant to the situation at hand. He would figure that out later.

Fortunately for Nylan, he had plenty of experience destroying the little monsters. He knew how they moved, knew the patterns they tended to fly. He saw its flickering motion out of the corner of his eye, tracked it for an instant, and did not wait. He lashed out with his stunrod. The weapon barely connected, but he felt the kick in his hand as the magic within triggered.

The tessila, stunned, began to fall. Looping flight interrupted, it tumbled out of the air to crash land onto the soft grass.

There was a gasp in the darkness, a shimmer on the air. The girl materialized not two feet away from Nylan. It was not J114, but one of the other seniors. That surprised him to stillness for half an instant. He could see in her face that she'd been coming for him. He'd been an instant away from his own death.

But her creature now lay in the grass, stunned. The girl's eyes had gone blank with fear and pain.

Nylan took one step to the side, lifted his booted foot. He stepped down, hard, directly on top of the fallen tessila.

Jey had just sent Phril into the crack when she heard the scream.

The dogs were upon her now. She'd blasted two of them to death, knowing that doing so revealed to the guards where she was. More and more guards were gathered atop the wall now. They stood shoulder to shoulder, short swords drawn, staring down into the darkness. They formed a barrier of metal and flesh between Jey and her freedom.

The remaining dogs were hanging back from the rosebush now that several of his companions were dead, but the orderlies were almost there. And they would have stunrods. Beyond that, Jey's ability to hold her passive echo spell was wavering. It would fall soon, whether she was prepared to be seen or not.

Jey blasted the life out of one more dog, then turned to grope for the handholds Kae had made in the wall. Again, she cleared her mind. She focused herself down to her grip on the stone, the need to climb, quick and sure.

It was possible the scream saved her life.

Jey had nearly reached the top of the wall when several things happened at once. First, she realized she could go no further. There was no way onto the top of the wall with all the men there. Second, a whole pack of orderlies reached the base of the wall and began beating at the rosebush and the surrounding air with their stunrods.

Third, the scream. It came from the other side of the wall. It was high and eerie in the night. Every guard, every orderly, every hound went momentarily still when they heard it.

The guards all turned and ran to the other side of the wall. Jey hauled herself upwards. As her arm reached onto the top, she lost her hold on her passive echo spell.

Below her, an orderly shouted. There was a sharp crack near her head and a spark in the darkness. She realized with sudden terror the man had thrown his stunrod. It had missed her by inches.

If one of those hits me, I will fall.

The thought galvanized Jey. She had no time to worry about the scream. She had to save her own skin.

With one final heave, she made the top of the wall. Several more stunrods clattered and sparked on the stones around her. She lurched forward, never pausing, to crash into the backs of two guards who were staring down over the other side of the wall. She knocked them aside before they could register her presence and threw herself out into the darkness beyond.

CHAPTER 7

Elle was not much prone to anger. Of the three seniors, she was the least deadly. While Elle excelled in situations that required diplomacy or deceit, violence had never come naturally to her. Her specialty was passive persuasion and other spells of the mind.

She'd climbed the wall quickly, avoided the guards, and leapt off the other side without stopping for a moment to consider what might be waiting at the bottom. None of them had thought beyond getting past the wall. It was a mistake Elle would regret for the rest of her life.

Elle held her passive bearing spell on the top of the wall, allowing her to land softly. Her tessila, Shai, darted like an arrow through the night. He came straight from the wall to cling to Elle's braid. As she transferred the brillbane bundle from where she'd gripped it between her teeth back to her hands, she felt their mingled relief at being together again.

She hadn't noticed Nylan. He'd been standing so still and quiet, tucked into the shadows at the base of the wall. She'd been preoccupied with the sounds of the baying hounds, the shouts of the guards.

Kae's tessila had always been the most aggressive of the three – the fastest to anger, the least inclined to sit still. While Elle's tessila clung to her body, heeding Elle's instructions to stay near and stay quiet, Kae's was a blur of movement in the dark night.

Elle saw Nylan as he stepped out of the shadows and struck. She saw Kae's tessila tumble out of the sky, saw Kae appear as her passive echo spell failed.

And she saw Nylan bring his boot down on top of her friend's tessila.

It had all happened too fast. In that instant, there was nothing Elle could do to prevent what happened. There was that horrible thump. Then, Kae crumpled. She collapsed into a limp heap on the grass.

She was dead. As dead as her tessila.

Elle screamed. The sound ripped out of her mouth in a kind of animal fury. She suddenly understood how Kae must have felt most of the time. Anger blasted through her like a hot tide. Her vision seemed to go red at the edges. Rage filled her, making her body tremble. She lost her hold on her passive echo spell. The look of terror in Nylan's eyes as she strode towards him made her smile.

◈

Jey fell through darkness. The torches atop the wall were smears of red light at the edges of her eyes. One of the guards gave a shout and pointed. An arrow sailed through the air towards her, but the aim was off. It had no chance of hitting.

Jey worked a passive bearing spell as she tumbled, but she could feel her fatigue. She'd drawn too hard on her reserves tonight. For one mad moment she thought the spell would fail. After all she had overcome, she would break her neck and back because she hadn't been able to contain the force of her own fall.

As it happened, Phril clawed his way free of the crack in the wall and flew to her as she fell. He caught onto her wrist. The small warmth of his body against her skin gave her new strength. She managed, at the last instant, to right herself. She landed heavily, but not fatally, in time to see Elle charge towards Nylan.

It took Jey a moment to grasp the situation. First, she saw Kae's body. The girl in the pale night dress was collapsed in the grass, as thoroughly dead as the orderly whose neck the girl had broken at the beginning of this insane night. Jey gave a silent gasp and froze in blank horror.

Kae was dead. Kae was dead, and even Jey, with all the advantages Phril gave her, could do nothing to change that fact.

Another arrow whizzed through the air, thrumming down to embed itself in the turf beside Jey with a hard thud. Jey tried to cast another passive echo spell, but she was too tired.

"Elle, come on." She barked the words as she started forward, casting a passive disruptor spell that knocked several more arrows off course.

But Elle wasn't listening. Jey turned to see her stalking Nylan like a cat. The Handler held a stunrod in one hand and a long, cruel knife in the other. He was taking careful backwards steps, facing Elle as she prowled towards him.

"Elle," Jey called again, "there's no time. We have to go."

Elle moved then. For a moment, Jey was transfixed by the sheer, fluid beauty of her friend's form. Elle darted in. Nylan swung the stunrod. The series of movements that happened next was too fast, too precise, too lovely to comprehend.

Elle blocked the swing. She did not use any magic. She stopped Nylan's wrist with her hands and broke it with a quick twist. Nylan gasped as the stunrod fell. But he still had the knife. Even as his face went pale with pain, he drove the weapon towards Elle's exposed side. Like Jey, her friend wore only the pale slip of her night dress.

Jey watched the incoming knife stroke with consternation, but Elle twisted to one side, danced past the incoming knife, and landed a kick on Nylan's knee. There was an audible crunch. Nylan stumbled, releasing a hoarse cry of pain.

The archers were getting organized now. Arrows fell in sheets. Jey could feel her fatigue, heavier and heavier as she wove her magic on the air. It was only a matter of time before one of the deadly shafts got through. Up at the main gate, there was the rattle of a chain. The hounds raised their voices in a chorus of excited baying as they surged out into the night. "Elle," she screamed. "Leave him. There's no time."

At last, her words penetrated. Elle looked up, taking in the flying arrows, the approaching dogs. As she turned her back on Nylan, she delivered one final kick, straight into his jaw. The Handler's head snapped back. He collapsed onto the grass next to Kae's body.

As Elle ran towards Jey, her face was smeared with tracks of tears. Jey felt her own eyes were hot. It felt wrong, leaving Kae lying in the grass. It felt like a betrayal. But they had no choice. Kae would have wanted them to go.

"We have to get into a deployment block," Jey said. She gestured at her skimpy dress. "We need some gear."

◈

Liam had found the tunnel in his eighth year at Tessili Academy.

He'd come upon it by accident. Unlike many of the professors he lived alongside, Liam was actually an academic. It was his studies, his work with magical text and theory, his curiosity about the history of the people who had once been able to wield magic, the Tessilari, that had gotten him noticed by the wrong people. Liam, young and curious and unafraid, had probed into places he should never have probed. He'd searched out information that had been systematically suppressed for centuries.

It wasn't until too late he realized he was playing with fire. He'd thought the histories he sought had merely faded, as histories will – falling out of collective memory with the passage of time. Never, in those days before his capture, had he so much as dreamed a place like Tessili Academy existed.

By the time he'd realized what he was risking, it had been too late.

Professor Liam had not left this island in the middle of the river in over two decades. In all likelihood, he would not escape this place through any means other than death. He'd spent a few angry years resisting, complaining, fighting. Then he'd gotten over it. He'd realized there was a library in the faculty compound, full of the exact kinds of texts he had used to seek out. He would have given his fortune to access such a place a few years before.

So, he'd given in. He'd rekindled his devotion to learning about magic. For fifteen years, he'd taught the Passive Magic course to the girls. He'd taught them to create the holdstones that allowed their lessons to penetrate their drug-fogged minds. He'd led them on maintenance walks, instructing them to replenish and strengthen the magic that held them prisoner. He'd taught them to create the brutal wands the orderlies carried to stun the students into submission as a last resort.

He'd done it all, year after year. He'd watched the girls grow up, grow distant and vague, and disappear.

Three times, he'd tried to wake one up. Each time, it had led to her premature death.

Now, Professor Liam stood at the window in his private chamber. The wall of the academy was alight with torches. He could hear the barking and baying of the hounds. He could see arrows glinting in the light of the torches as they fell. He'd come back to the faculty campus, running as fast as he could, dodging around frantic orderlies until he'd reached the store room that led to the strange slit in the wall that led to another slit and another slit that led at last to a tunnel that went below the wall and ended behind a bookshelf in the faculty library. He didn't know how long Jey's magic had stayed with him, but if anyone had seen him they hadn't let on.

Liam didn't know who'd made the tunnel. He didn't know if anyone other than him knew of its existence. He himself had never used it since the day he'd noticed a draft seeping out from below a section of shelves and gone exploring.

If other faculty were awake, they were keeping to their chambers. Like Liam, each person here was a prisoner. When Liam had been offered the choice between the loss of his freedom and the loss of his life, he'd seen no alternative. The other men here were all the same. Though they never spoke of their past lives, though they never discussed the errors they'd made that had landed them here, Liam suspected he was not the only one who dreamed of seeing the academy fall.

Outside, the night was bright with silver moonlight. Liam stared at the short bridge where the cobbled road passed over the river. He stared at that place because it was the last choke point, the final spot the girls might be caught. The academy was built on an island in the heart of the widest river in the land. A single fortified bridge connected this place to the mainland. He stared, even though he knew it would take a small miracle for the girls to reach the bridge at all.

The challenges the girls were up against seemed insurmountable. The escape from the cloister, dodging hounds and orderlies, making it through and over the massive wall and past the guards on top. Although the seniors were strong in comparison to the other students, Liam alone, perhaps, understood how stunted these girls were. They could cast only a small number of spells. They were easily run to the end of their strength. If they made it over the wall at all, they would be too exhausted to conceal themselves any longer.

Liam heard a scream. It was a girl's scream, full of rage and despair. His heart sank at the sound. He could see activity around the gatehouse, could see the great gates swinging open. He clenched his fists on the windowsill as a pack of hounds poured out into the night.

The sighthounds came first, graceful and fast on their long legs. They raced away into the darkness. The scenthounds came next. They were blocky things with swaying jowls. They ran with their noses to the ground, weaving back and forth, trying to catch a scent.

Orderlies came behind, clutching stunrods.

Once the dogs and men were through, the gates swung shut again.

For a while, then, all was quiet. The voices of the hounds grew distant. The activity on the wall stilled. Liam stared out into the night, returning his attention to the bridge.

It seemed an age passed. Liam strained and stared, his heart pounding, his mouth dry.

Then, at last, he saw them – two girls, clad all in black. They moved from behind the deployment blocks and made for the bridge. There was a guardhouse there, the final barrier.

The girls moved with more grace than even the hounds, long legs moving in an efficient rhythm as they gained the stone path. Liam glanced back, hoping to see a third. But there were only two.

One of them scaled the wall, moving with a liquid grace that took Liam's breath away. Although he'd seen them in class, they'd been hampered then, inhibited by their inefficient access to their own memories. Now his breath caught as the girl, dark hair flying, moved along the wall, mowing down the surprised guards like a scythe cuts wheat.

The other waited, standing guard at the foot of the bridge. Her long hair was pale in the moonlight. She stood there, on the threshold of freedom, and her head turned in Liam's direction.

In the distance, a hound bayed. The first girl finished her work atop the wall and dropped out of sight. A moment later, the gatehouse portcullis lifted open.

The light-haired girl stood a moment longer. Although she was too far away for him to be sure, she seemed to be looking directly at Liam. It was as if she could see him in his window, watching.

Then, Jey raised one hand in farewell. She turned and pulled up her hood, becoming nothing but another shadow in the night. She crossed the bridge and disappeared.

◈

Elle and Jey ran side by side. They'd found one of the deployment blocks open and moved through it in quick efficiency. They'd donned the dark leathers and cloaks they wore on their opportunities. The leathers were both flexible and sturdy, reinforced with a magical weave. The cloaks had pockets. Jey and Elle divided the brillbane husks, strapped on a weapons belt each, and fled into the night.

No longer half naked, no longer unarmed, the girls were unstoppable. Elle neutralized the guards at the gatehouse before they knew they were under attack.

As Jey stood at the base of the bridge, waiting to make sure they weren't attacked from the grounds, she noticed the hulking shape of the faculty campus. Many of the windows were ablaze with light. Figures stood in the windows. Most of the profiles seemed to be straining towards the academy.

But one man was looking straight at the gate. Jey's heart lurched when she realized she'd been seen, but then her anxiety vanished when she recognized the familiar outline. It was Liam, leaning against his windowsill. Jey felt a flare of relief. He'd made it back, somehow.

That knowledge tucked itself in opposite the weight in Jey's soul left by Kae's death, a buoying shard of hope in this dark night.

Behind her, the portcullis rattled open. Jey found herself grinning. There had been no need for Elle to open the gate. Jey could have climbed over quite easily. Her friend had done this as a final insult, a goad, a comment on how thoroughly the girls had overcome the barriers their captors had used to contain them.

Jey looked towards Professor Liam for one more moment. There were so many things she did not know. She was seized by the sudden desire to go back, to break down the door to the faculty campus, to bring him with them.

But there was no time. The hounds were baying again. They would have found Kae's body by now. They were on the trail. Even once the girls crossed the bridge, the hounds would stay after them.

But she was no longer worried. She and Elle, together, could hide their trail. Soon, they would recover from their fatigue. They had been trained to move undetected through the countryside. Jey and Elle had done it many times before.

No, they could not take Professor Liam now. Jey knew that. As Elle, behind her, hissed, "Come on," Jey raised an arm and held her hand aloft, a silent goodbye.

But as she turned and fell into step beside Elle, she promised herself they would be back. She and Elle would return, someday, to Tessili Academy. And they would see this place never held another prisoner, ever again.

For now, though, she had more prosaic concerns to face. The two girls trotted across the bridge, shoulder to shoulder, listening to the lazy ripple of the quiet river in the still night. They reached land, stepped off the bridge, and Jey spared one final glance at the island, distant now and ablaze with light.

She felt the soft pressure of Elle's hand in hers. As if her friend could read her thoughts, she whispered, "We'll come back. We'll come back when we're stronger, when we know more. And we'll free them all."

Jey nodded, thinking of Kae, who would never be free. She turned, dashing hot tears from her eyes. Then she took a deep breath. She and Elle, hand in hand, ran off the road and into the night.

Tessili Rogue

Chronicles of the Tessilari : Book II

Robin Stephen

Ever since he'd been a boy, Lokim had wanted to leave the Valley of Mist.

As a child, he'd tested the boundaries. He would make forays into the gray, swirling fog that encircled the valley. He'd keep going as his vision went soft, until the air grew muffled and chill. As the world faded from view his heart would begin to pound with fear. He would turn back when he was one step away from losing his memory of which direction led home.

When he'd been older, he'd made a more serious attempt. One bright day he'd slipped into the fog and begun to walk. He'd moved ahead with determination, going further than he'd ever gone before. He'd walked and walked, certain with every step he'd make it, that the air would clear and he'd see … he'd see the world.

Except, he hadn't. After marching forward for an hour, he'd thought the fog seemed thinner. He'd hurried ahead, eyes, straining, only to find himself emerging from the mists in the precise spot he'd entered them. High Mage Agina had been waiting for him, eyes flinty, firm mouth set in a hard line.

Lokim had known better than to try again.

For a time, he'd given up. He'd contented himself with watching for rovers. Every time a group came in from their travels, he would ask for stories. Most of them developed a sort of annoyed fondness for the boy. They would answer questions if they had nothing better to do. But the rovers never stayed for long.

When, years later, Lokim had his moment and succeeded in passing beyond the veil, he'd thought himself prepared. He'd mastered the skills the rovers said he would need to survive. He thought he understood the ways of the people he would find beyond the veil. Like all the Tessilari, he'd studied the histories. He knew about the Betrayal and all that had followed.

He'd been prepared to find monsters. What he'd discovered was people.

◆

Shai was not happy. Jey could feel his rage, boiling out of the tessila's small body like dull heat, filling her with the desire to let him go.

Jey was ignoring him. Or, at least, she was trying to. It wasn't easy. The small creature lay within the grip of her left hand, delicate wings pinned to his small body, purple head protruding from between her index finger and thumb, tail lashing beyond her pinkie. Unlike Phril, Shai had a set of sharp spikes along the base of his skull. Jey's hand now bled where he'd used these to stab her. It was tricky, holding him tight enough to prevent his escape, but not so tight as to do him any harm.

Phril was also not happy. He did not like Jey to have contact with any tessila other than himself. He crouched on her wrist a few inches away from Shai. He was coiled into an angry knot, wings flared, hissing at the other tessila every time he stabbed Jey with the spikes.

Jey was trying to read. Holdam had loaned her a text on the methods of preparing soft cheeses. It was an old book, well worn, with many of Holdam's own notes written in the margins.

After her long day working in the cheesery, Jey was exhausted. It was well past midnight. She glanced with longing at the two tidy beds that stood on the other side of the small room. They were both neatly made, plain woolen blankets tucked in, down pillows fluffed. *I could lie down for just a moment.*

Jey squashed the thought. She knew better than to give in to fatigue. Her duty was to hold Shai. Shai did not want to be held. It would take only a moment of carelessness for him to escape her grasp. And that would be a disaster.

Jey rubbed her forehead with her free hand. She moved her small dish of oil with its wick and flame closer to the book. The spidery handwriting on the page seemed to swim before her eyes.

There was a tap on the chamber door.

Jey jerked in her seat, resisting the impulse to fling Shai from her hand, launch herself across the room, and draw the two long knives from where they lay hidden beneath her mattress. She spat out a quiet curse, cast two quick passive echo spells—one on Phril, one on Shai—instructed Phril to hold still so the spell would actually work, and said in a mild tone, "Come in."

Jey turned in her chair. Her heart was pounding. Her desire to arm herself grew intolerably intense as the latch clicked and the door swung inward, spilling a little more light into the dim room.

Biala poked her head around the door. Her long braid, shot with gray, hung down before one shoulder. Her expression, lit by the candle she held, was friendly.

She looked into the room. "I saw your light. I admire your thirst for knowledge, Jey, but you young people should not neglect your rest."

Jey blinked in what she hoped looked like abstracted bemusement, gazing at the inky night outside the window. "I didn't realize it had grown so late."

But Biala's brow had furrowed as she took in the rest of the room. Her mouth compressed into a small frown. "But where is Elle?"

Jey felt fatigue bloom through her as Shai increased his squirming in a sudden renewed bid for freedom. She was so tired. If she couldn't talk her way out of this, she'd have to cast a passive persuasion spell on Biala. Passive persuasions were Elle's specialty, not hers. It was the last thing she needed.

Jey stood, easing out of her chair and moving a few steps closer to the woman and her candle. She tried to do so in a way that suggested nothing more than a desire to stretch her legs. "She couldn't sleep, so she went for a walk." She made her tone mild and lazy, as if it was the most normal thing in the world for an 18 year old girl to wander outside, alone, at night, in the dead of winter.

Biala's eyes narrowed further. "A walk?" she said. "At midnight?"

Jey was about the answer, but a sudden stab of pain in her hand caused her to almost cry out. Shai had flung his head against her hand with the greatest force he'd managed yet. The spikes on the back of his head bit into the base of her index finger. Phril, stirred to anger, leapt forward. He would have attacked the other tessila had Jey not cupped her free hand over Shai to protect him. Shai proceeded to pull his spikes free and drive them in again.

Something of her pain and distraction must have shown on Jey's face, because Biala's eyes softened. She let out a small chuckle, looking again at Jey, the oil light, the book, the two empty beds. She winked and turned, leaving the astonished Jey to stare at her back. "Delari knows, there's nothing like a full moon to inspire a late night rendezvous. I wonder who the lucky young man is."

Jey didn't answer, and Biala withdrew behind the door. "See you both tomorrow," the woman said. "But warn Elle there will be no lessening of duties for those who choose romance over sleep."

Jey, heart pounding, stood still until the latch clicked. Then she dropped the passive echo spells and glared down at Phril, who was trying to claw his way past her protective hand to get at Shai. "Stop it," she hissed. "Phril. That is enough." She made no attempt to shield him from the frustration and annoyance she was feeling.

Phril, suddenly sulky, flew across the room to alight on the windowsill, seething with resentment. Jey removed her protective hand and looked down at Shai, who was glaring up at her, his sharp face smeared with her blood. Jey sank back into her chair. "Both of you need to calm down. You should know the drill by now."

But they did not know the drill. Tessili were famous for their intractability, but it seemed to Jey both Shai and Phril had been increasingly volatile lately.

She knew Phril was, in part, reacting to her own stress. The truth was, Jey hated these nights – the nights Elle crept off through the darkness to break into Tessili Academy.

◆

Lokim tracked the girl with relative ease. Though she moved through the night with the grace and silence of a hunting cat, Lokim had gotten used to her ways. He knew the way she walked, the places she stopped to watch for pursuit, even the signature of her magic. For the last six months, he'd followed her every time she left the cheesery.

For the last six months, time after time, he'd tried to gather the courage to approach her. But he never had.

The girl, Elle, she was called, paused before stepping into the shallow stream. She would now walk in it for a time, making it more difficult for the hounds to follow her scent. He winced as he watched her step into the cold water. The night was bitter. Shards of ice had formed along the edges of the stream. Elle waded along, her dark leathers soaking up the chill water. Lokim waited until she was all but lost in the darkness before hopping to the other side, keeping his own feet dry.

About a hundred yards down the stream an old, gnarled tree grew above the water. Elle paused and jumped, grabbing a long branch with her gloved hands. She dangled for a moment, then pulled herself up. She moved along the branch and down the trunk. Feet once more on the ground, she broke into a steady jog, heading towards the outskirts of Deramor and the cheesery where she now lived.

Lokim let out an admiring breath. He'd never seen anyone so graceful, so smooth, so slender and yet so strong. This was one of several spots Elle and Jey used the stream to confuse the dogs and throw them off the trail. So far, it had always worked.

Lokim waited until Elle was almost out of sight. He was about to move again, to follow, when he saw something. It was a faint blur, a shifting in the shadows at the corner of his eye.

He froze, listening. The flowing of the cold stream was a silver chuckle in the still night. He waited.

Another girl emerged from the darkness. She, too, moved with the intent grace of a predator. But unlike Elle, she was not familiar to him. Although Lokim had never seen her before, she wore the same dark leathers as Elle, the same twin knives strapped to her hips. She did not wet her feet, but hopped the stream and paused for a moment, listening.

Lokim's hand flew to the knife on his belt, but the girl was intent on one thing. She continued, tracking Elle as surely as Lokim was.

As the girl disappeared into the dark woods, Bliz swept in a sudden, agitated loop around Lokim's head. Lokim held out a hand and the orange tessila alighted. He ran a finger along the sharp edge of her chin. "Shush, brilliant one. It's ok." He said these words in the barest of whispers as he began to move, tracking the girl who tracked Elle.

What did it mean? Lokim had developed some theories in the last months, but he had no answers. He didn't know why Jey and Elle returned to a place they appeared to loath, time after time, but he had his guesses. Now, it appeared, their visits had been noticed.

Around him, the woodland that stretched between the walled island and the outlying settlements of the country's capital was empty and silent. For six months,

Lokim had told himself he would make contact, he would talk to them. Tomorrow.

But now it seemed tomorrow might be too late.

As Lokim walked, tracking the ghost of the movement that was the second girl, he seemed to hear High Mage Agina's voice, speaking in his head. *Do not trust your ally. He will betray you. Allies are more dangerous than enemies, for they wear a false face. The only true bond is blood.*

These words had held him immobile for six months. They'd held him back, kept him cowering in the shadows, waiting, watching, hoping for some way to know if it was safe to reveal himself. He didn't know if these girls would turn out to be allies or enemies, or a little bit of both.

Now, he realized with a sudden sense of clarity, revealing himself would never be safe. Nothing he'd done since he'd left the Valley of the Mist was safe. But that did not mean it wasn't worth doing.

In the darkness, Lokim drew his knife.

About the Author

Robin has always been enamored with magic.

When she was a child, that meant reading books. When she was a slightly older child, it meant trying to write her own. She produced her first attempt at a fantasy story at the age of 10. It was an unintentionally blatant (and considerably less well executed) rip-off of *The Lion, the Witch, and the Wardrobe.*

Fortunately for everyone, Robin's stories have gotten a little more original over the years. She currently lives in Iowa City, where she hangs out with her husband, trains horses, and writes.

learn more at robinstephen.com

Robin also writes contemporary western romance

If you like horses, love stories, and the desert, explore Robin's work under the pen name Stefani Wilder. Her book, *A Man Who Rides* is available now.

see stefaniwilder.com for details